Last Waltz on Wild Horse

A WESTERN QUARTET

T. T. Flynn

CENTER POINT LARGE PRINT
THORNDIKE, MAINE

This Center Point Large Print edition
is published in the year 2016 in conjunction with
Golden West Literary Agency.

The text of this Large Print edition is unabridged.
In other aspects, this book may vary
from the original edition.

Set in 16-point Times New Roman type.

ISBN: 978-1-62899-877-1 (hardcover)
ISBN: 978-1-62899-881-8 (paperback)

Library of Congress Cataloging-in-Publication Data

Names: Flynn, T. T., author. | Flynn, T. T., author. Showdown in blood.
Title: Last waltz on wild horse : a western quartet / T. T. Flynn.
Description: Center Point Large Print edition. | Thorndike, Maine :
Center Point Large Print, 2016. | ©2008
Identifiers: LCCN 2015042675| ISBN 9781628998771 (hardcover : alk.
paper) | ISBN 9781628998818 (pbk. : alk. paper)
Subjects: LCSH: Western stories. | Large type books.
Classification: LCC PS3556.L93 A6 2016 | DDC 813/.54—dc23
LC record available at http://lccn.loc.gov/2015042675

Printed and bound in Great Britain
by TJ International Ltd, Padstow, Cornwall

Table of Contents

Showdown in Blood

T. T. Flynn completed this story in late 1947. It was purchased for *Dime Western* by editor Mike Tilden on January 19, 1948 and the author was paid $454. The story was retitled "Hot Gun Town" when it was published in the May, 1948 issue. For its appearance here the author's original title has been restored.

I

It started on the St. Louis levee, two boys fighting furiously among the great piles of freight, before a whooping audience of steamboat hands, roust-abouts, teamsters, top-hatted townsmen, and brawny immigrant passengers attracted by the excitement. Perhaps it started long before, as fate. Who knows such things? Who dares to answer?

Bud Keyhoe was the bigger, looking older than his ten years, a solid-muscled boy with a bold shock of yellow hair and white, strong teeth. Trace Ballard was nine, shorter, chunkier, with black hair. A swing of Bud's fist knocked him down again.

Trace rolled toward the circle of spectators and heard the bawled warning of a big Wisconsin log raftsman.

"Git up, young 'un! He'll stomp you!"

Trace rolled violently.

Bud's bare, calloused heel missed his head. "You're licked!" Bud yelled. "Say you're licked! Say I'm right!"

Trace scrambled away and lurched up. He wanted to yell back but the words clogged in his throat. It was always this way in anger or a fight. Everything stayed bottled up inside.

Bud plunged at him.

"Look out, young 'un!" the raftsman shouted. "He's got a rock!"

Keyhoe smashed Ballard above the ear with the rock.

When Trace opened his eyes, the bearded rafts-man had him down by the river's edge, slopping water on his face from cupped hands.

"He's gone, boy," the raftsman said as Trace started up groggily. "I run him off. What was you young roosters sparrin' about?"

"He helped my kid brother Wes and me haul packages to the *North Queen* in our hand wagon," Trace panted. "Bud wanted half the money. Said he was the biggest and had a right to half."

"He git it?"

"No! But Bud wants Wes to run off with him next year. Me, too. Bud says he means to own a hundred freight wagons hauling West and have lots of gold. I told him he wouldn't. I wouldn't take it back!"

"He fought you over it, huh?"

"Yep."

"Well, now, mebbe he's right."

A red flannel shirt sleeve was rolled back on the hairy arm that pointed to the freight going on and off the steamboats as far as they could see along the levee. The bull teams and mule teams. The heavy freight wagons and bowed canvas tops of immigrant wagons, fancy-dressed passengers, and work-worn women with children tagging along behind them. All the exciting, busy levee life Trace was never to forget. Nor did Trace forget what the logger from the north woods said.

"Look at it, son! The whole world's movin' West! Ain't only Saint Looey here. We see it when the rafts come downriver. They're crossin' everywhere. Comin' from God knows what all. Wimmenfolks. Kids, too. Know what that means, boy?"

"Freight," Trace guessed.

"You ain't no knothead, boy. Wimmen an' kids mean homes to stay in. Stuff they got to have. The boats can git it up the Missouri a ways. Someday there'll be a railroad out beyond Jefferson. Out over the prairies. God knows when. But the wagons ain't a-waitin'. There'll be more freight each year. More wimmen an' kids. This here Bud you tangled with is a good-lookin', fast-thinkin' young rooster. Might be he'll grow big an' have them freight wagons and gold."

"Wes thinks so," Trace muttered. He picked up a small, flat rock and paused, frowning as he thought hard. "If the railroads go West, they'll carry all the freight and gold, won't they?"

"Every danged load an' dollar of it, boy. Fast an' cheap. Beats a crawlin' bull wagon or stage-coach all holler."

"Wes will follow Bud," Trace said gravely. "He

always does. Wes is stubborn, too, unless it's Bud telling him. We don't have folks, except Aunt Maggie. Wes don't like her much. He'll run off when Bud says so."

"Off to git a hundred freight wagons full of gold, huh?" The big raftsman chuckled. "An' what'll you do, boy?"

Trace skipped the flat rock out under the guards of the nearest steamboat—and another entry went into the book of fate. Or perhaps it was there already.

"I'll help build railroads and carry all the freight," Trace said dreamily.

He wiped a sleeve of his hickory shirt over his wet face and winced as he touched the swelling where the rock had struck.

"Bud'll get the freight wagons and gold from Wes," he guessed. "All of it. That's how Bud does. He's got to have everything, 'cause he's smartest and strongest. Bud's got to be that way if it kills him."

"Or kills the other feller," the raftsman suggested with amusement. "Bud's a fightin' cock. Smart and greedy. He'll git ahead, I see."

"He's never made me say I'm licked," Trace said darkly. "Makes him mad when I don't tell him." Trace wiped his face again. "I'm learning Bud's tricks. Someday I'll lick him good. Bud knows it. I can tell."

"Well, now . . ." The raftsman was laughing

in his beard as his big hand slapped Trace's shoulder. "You got guts, boy. I'll say that. Mean to lick him someday, huh?"

"Sure," Trace said, not hesitating. "Bud knows it, too. You watch."

"I'd log a winter on the Black River to see it," the raftsman said. He clouted farewell on Trace's shoulder. "But watch him, young 'un. He'll have new tricks."

The big logger from Wisconsin's Black River never saw it. His entry was on another page, balanced in the Yazoo swamps below Vicksburg, when Sherman's men were hurled back from the Chickasaw Bluffs.

Years later, as a train rolled through the early prairie night toward Denton City, the new boom camp at the end of westward-reaching track, Trace thought again of the bearded raftsman. A man named Keyhoe had been mentioned by Susan Croston, who was traveling West with an aunt to join her father, Colonel Croston, commanding at Fort Denton, near the railroad town.

"I knew a Walter Keyhoe, ma'am," Trace said, watching the restless lamplight in Susan's fine brown hair. "We called him Bud. He ran away to be a freighter." Trace smiled reflectively. "And to get stacks of gold. I wonder . . ."

Miss Agatha Croston, the colonel's gray-haired, unmarried sister, stirred restlessly beside the window. "This Mister Walter Keyhoe did mention, sir, when he was in Kansas City, that freighting was one of his interests. A most successful and interesting young gentleman."

"He had yellow hair," Trace recalled.

Expression could run lightly on Susan Croston's face. All day Trace had watched her face: smiling, eager, pensive. Now he watched her quick interest. "Mister Keyhoe must be the boy you knew," Susan decided.

"Did he mention a Wes Ballard?" Trace asked her.

"I don't think he did," Susan said.

"Wes is my brother. They ran away together. They were to be partners," Trace said. He fell silent, looking again at the lamplight in Susan's hair, thinking of Wes and Bud.

Two seats back in the coach, across the aisle, where Trace himself belonged, solemn amusement held Long Jack Edwards and Hardy Wilcox as they watched him with the ladies. Trace leveled a restrained glare at the two—and then listened intently as the shrill engine whistle signaled for hand brakes.

"Why are we stopping?" Miss Agatha asked with a thin, ascending note of alarm. "Could it be Indians?"

"Not likely, so near Fort Denton and your brother's troopers, ma'am," Trace said calmly.

But he came to his feet in the aisle, holding to

the seat back against the jolting slack of speed. "If there's any trouble," he said on second thought, "get down on the floor."

He smiled reassuringly at the mute query in Susan's look, and moved down the aisle to Long Jack and Hardy Wilcox. Both men were on their feet. The whistle still blew frantically.

"Well?" Long Jack asked.

"Better get out on the platform," Trace decided. "I'll take the front end."

He pulled a leather valise from the luggage rack, opened it quickly on the seat, and took out a belt and holstered gun. He was checking the loaded cylinder when the train made a shuddering stop and a burst of gunfire up toward the engine told its story.

The train was carrying construction workers for Curby Matson's swelling payrolls, and dance-hall girls and gamblers for their pay money. Hide hunters were headed West to outfit at Denton City for the winter buffalo kill. Miners, cowmen, settlers, dark-skinned New Mexicans, and merchants would continue on West from the end of track by wagon freighters and stagecoach.

For the most part they knew what to do now. One man, his face pressed against the window, called out as Trace ran forward in the aisle. "They ain't Indians! That's a white man just rode by!"

Trace caught the faint jar of booted feet leaping

15

up the car steps at the front end. He stopped and gave a last pull to the heavy gun belt he was buckling outside his coat.

The masked man kicked the door open and stood behind a threatening revolver. He was breathing hard. "You folks won't be bothered!" he called through the blue handkerchief mask. "Sit still!"

He saw Trace's move and fanned a quick shot. Trace's drawn gun prolonged the shattering report. The man folded slowly in the doorway; he was falling to the left as he vanished.

As Trace ran out on the platform, a woman back in the coach cried for help. He had a twist of fear that Colonel Croston's daughter or sister had been killed, but had no time to look. A gun flash reached toward him from the prairie night.

II

Trace heard the bullet rip into the coach wood behind him. He went off the platform in a long jump and took two steps before he dropped, chest down, on the short, dry grass.

The masked gunman died below the coach steps as Trace lay watchfully out beyond him, trying to see clearly the man on horseback who had fired the last shot. The same man drove another bullet within a foot of Trace's shoulder, kicking dirt against his face. Offside the rear of the coach a gun blurted from the buffalo grass. Still farther out a second gun drove another shot. The dimly seen rider went down, evidently dragging the reins. His horse stood uneasily.

"You hurt, Ballard?" Wilcox called from the direction in which the first gun had hammered.

"No," Trace said, rising. "There's a payroll in the express car."

A hard-ridden horse swung well out around them toward the head of the train. The fast beat of another galloping animal went forward on the other side of the coaches. Long Jack's cautious voice lifted out beyond Wilcox.

"They're in the express car. The rest are keeping out on the prairie in the dark. Plenty of them, too. How about it?"

A burst of gunfire sounded well out from the express car. Trace went close against the ground. "More of them than I thought," he decided reluctantly. "Stay down."

He understood the regret in Hardy's comment. "I hate to start something and see it thin out this way."

"We started to Denton City," Trace said shortly.

Passengers had been hastily putting out the aisle lamps in the coaches. The moonless night came hard against the grass. Lights in the express car also went out. The engine headlight evidently had been shot out. A few glowing sparks whirled up from the stack; wind brought the rankness of engine smoke.

The boiler safety valve popped in a roaring plume of pale steam. It was just possible to make out blurred movements near the express car. The steam stopped blowing. Voices speaking with low intensity at the express car gave way quickly to the hard run of horses retreating south, toward Indian Territory.

Trace stood up, listening. Long Jack and Hardy joined him, and Trace said: "Let's see what they left."

Two dead buffalo piled on the track had stopped the train. The fireman had a shoulder wound. Two men were dead in the express car.

"They knew better than to watch what I was stopping for," the engineer said glumly, looking in at the bodies. "Got picked off in the door-way just as we stopped. Joe Black was married, too."

"Two more back there to ride with them," Trace said. He added regretfully: "Not enough."

Aisle lights in the coaches were being cautiously relit. Armed men were emerging belatedly and gathering around the bodies.

A second saddled horse was found ground-tied. Hardy and Long Jack climbed on the horses and rode to drag the dead buffalo off the track. Trace had help in putting the bodies in the express car. He learned that the woman who had cried out was the wife of a Colorado-bound settler. Her husband had been hit in the neck by the bullet that had missed Trace.

The unsaddled horses were turned out on the prairie. The brakeman took the place of the wounded fireman, and the train went on.

Trace was the last one back in the coach. He stood for a moment inside the door, a thoughtful, almost remote figure. He was of medium build. There was a black curliness in his hair and stubborn strength in the line of his jaw.

He unbuckled the gun belt slowly and held it dangling as he walked to the clutter of passengers in the aisle, where the wounded man was leaning back, neck swathed in a blood-soaked cloth.

The entire coach watched him come to that seat. There was a silent shifting in the crowded aisle to let him stand where the wife sat intently watching her husband. She was past her youth. Trace sensed in her the plain dignity of inner strength that was taking her West to a new life.

"I'm sorry this happened, ma'am," he said soberly.

She turned her head. "It needn't have happened. The man said he'd not hurt anyone. You started the trouble."

"So I did," Trace agreed. "There was a big payroll in the express car I hoped to save."

She said—"Payroll!"—on a soft note of tearing grief, and looked stonily back at her husband.

The silence around them weighed in behind her words as Trace went on in the aisle, lurching a little with the sway of the car. He saw Susan Croston watching his approach. Susan's aunt's thin mouth set distrustfully as he paused, asking: "Are you ladies all right?"

Susan nodded, her look a little puzzled, as if seeking in him the same man who had talked smilingly all day, but not finding him at all.

Agatha Croston leaned forward indignantly. "We might have been killed, sir, thanks to your acting like a desperado yourself!"

"I suppose it might seem that way to some folks."

"You killed a man when there was no need to!"

"I thought the need was there. I'm sorry you don't agree."

He was starting on when Susan said quickly: "I'm sure it must have been necessary."

"Thank you," Trace said.

He went on back and sat opposite his companions. Long Jack, a spare, almost elegant man with drooping black mustaches and a massive gold chain across a blue-and-yellow flowered silken waistcoat, spoke idly. "Folks out this way seem to be against killing a man . . . until after he kills you."

"They may be right," Trace said shortly.

He saw Wilcox's quick, searching stare, and met it. There was something in Hardy's eyes that never warmed. Hardy's mustache was brown, against a rounded face that was always placid. Only the eyes, the blue, cold eyes, set Wilcox apart.

Trace let the question wait in Hardy's look and turned his face to the night outside the dusty window. Reflected in the glass, he saw the look Hardy gave Long Jack.

He let that look stand, too, with all it might imply in the days ahead for the three of them, and sat silently until the engine whistle and slackening speed marked the final mile into Denton City and the end of rail.

Only then Trace stood up, buckled the gun belt under his coat, and went forward to the two ladies, offering his assistance off the train.

"We will sit here until Colonel Croston comes for us," Miss Agatha said stiffly. Susan smiled up at him despite her aunt's disapproval. "Thank you for your kindness, Mister Ballard. If Mister Keyhoe visits the fort, shall I speak about you?"

"I wish you would, ma'am," Trace said. Bud Keyhoe would visit the fort, he guessed, as he went back for his valise and rifle. Her aunt would see to it. Bud was still getting the best of everything. What had Wes got since he'd run away? Trace wondered.

He had not been to Denton City, but he knew how it would be, and it was all there when he stepped down by the plank shack that served for a station.

Not long ago this had been the blue distance of empty buffalo prairie where wagon trains and stages had lifted dust in their slow passing. Trace threaded the confusion alongside the train and walked out alone into the ribald, lantern-spotted night.

It was like other railhead towns he had known. Long side tracks out on the prairie held cars loaded with supplies. Iron rails, cross-ties, boxes, barrels, and kegs were stacked high under the stars.

The town itself was a place of tents, shacks, and a few larger, portable structures. A place of saloons and dance halls, horse and mule and wagon corrals, the fenced yards of buffalo hide traders, and stage and wagon freight stations for the traffic West beyond railroad iron.

He turned from the town and presently located the rebuilt boxcar that served as a rolling office for Curby Matson, the new construction chief for the next spurt of track laying.

Curby looked with a frown from a battered roll-top desk and a gaunt man standing there with a sheaf of papers. He saw it was Trace and bounced to his feet with welcome, snatching a dead cigar stump from the side of his mouth.

"Did you get my telegram about Colonel Croston's womenfolks?" Curby asked.

"I did what I could for them."

"Good! We need the colonel's good will."

Curby rocked restlessly on his toes, a compact, muscular man. He was ambitious, energetic. Matson would never pause while there was empty country calling for railroad. Trace understood him; Trace had something of the same long vision.

"How many men did you bring?" Curby asked hopefully.

"Two," Trace said, eyeing the gaunt man beside the desk.

"Only two?" Curby exploded. He held back further comment and indicated the gaunt man. "Otto Soderholm, our paymaster. Otto, this is Trace Ballard. Worked under me on the Union Pacific. Been East since then getting some new engineer learning. He's replacing Darcy."

Soderholm looked startled and seemed to see Trace for the first time. He was a harried-looking man, as if work under Matson was too heavy. "I'll put your name on the payroll," he told Trace.

"You'd better telegraph for more payroll money," Trace said, putting down the valise. "The train was held up."

Matson hurled the frayed cigar to the dusty floor. His oaths were fluent and bitter. "That money was shipped two days early. Only a few knew it was on the train. Couldn't you stop it at all?"

"Too many of them. We killed a couple. After that it seemed best to wait."

A flush came to Curby's face. "I haven't time to wait. Over three thousand men on the payroll now, including the forward grading camps. They won't work without pay days on time. They aren't working, anyway. I started this job behind schedule. It's falling further behind. You should have brought ten men. Twenty would have been better."

Trace flushed, too. "I didn't want this job, Curby. I want to build a railroad."

"What do you think I'm trying to do?" Curby sat at the desk again and spoke more calmly. "The town is out of hand, Trace. Hide hunters are outfitting here. Freighters and stages are meeting us from the west and southwest. A few cattle drives are already here. Soldiers from the fort make it worse. Our payrolls are fattening outlaws and gamblers instead of getting rail laid. Some of my best men have been killed." Curby shook his head sadly. "You brought two men."

"Hardy Wilcox and Long Jack Edwards," Trace said.

Curby's square hand groped into a desk drawer and came out with a fresh cigar, which he held forgotten. "Wilcox and Edwards," he repeated, and sat motionless.

Soderholm cleared his throat. "I can't keep losing payroll money. Something has to be . . ." He stopped, realizing neither man was listening.

"Can you do it before pay day?" Curby asked.

"A month isn't enough," Trace said irritably. "You know it."

"Five days," Curby said, dropping a fist on the desk. "Get this town straightened out before pay day, so my men won't be slugged, robbed, cheated, shot, and made useless for days. I've got to have that to build railroad fast. I agreed to build fast. Do it, Trace, or you're no good to me."

Trace picked up the valise. "Is there a wagon freighter and businessman here named Walter Keyhoe?"

"Got a hide yard by the Missouri corral," Curby said shortly. He bent forward. "What about the job?"

"Ask me after pay day," Trace said. "You know I wouldn't have this, if it didn't go with laying iron."

"You went through it on the U.P.," Curby

reminded. "That's why I thought of you. Give me reasonable law and order quick and you'll help build more railroad than the spike gangs. There's a room for you at the Travelers House." Curby took a cigar box from the bottom desk drawer, dumped an assortment of law badges on the desk, and held out three. Trace picked up another badge drilled by a bullet hole a little off center. "Who wore this?"

"John Darcy," Curby said with some reluctance. "I sent for you after Darcy was shot. Don't know why I kept his badge."

"Who did it?"

"Nobody knows. Darcy had his gun out when he was found behind the Buffalo Corral."

"What's that?"

"Biggest bar in town. The worst," Curby said. He sat scowling at his thoughts. "I don't think Darcy had a chance, even if his gun was out."

"Why?"

"His gun wasn't fired. It was put into his hand or Darcy pulled it as he was dropping." Curby's scowl lingered. "Too much easy money, Trace. The bad ones are here from everywhere to get it. Still coming. It's getting worse fast. We'll have to make our own law quick, like we've done before."

Trace nodded and tossed one badge back and kept the punctured one. He looked back from the doorway at the worried paymaster. "There's no good place down in the Nations to spend your

26

stolen payroll," he said thoughtfully. "I'll look for it here in town in a day or so."

He left Soderholm's silence behind, guessing the gaunt man had little faith. The clamor of the boom camp reached through the night at him and he walked into it.

Curby Matson's men crowded everywhere, noisy and exuberant. Buffalo hunters in fringed buckskins, muleskinners, and bullwhackers jostled immigrant men headed farther West, who had never seen anything like this and showed it. The few cowmen Trace saw seemed to be keeping with their own kind. The dim night pulsed with a kind of edgy excitement in which anything could and did happen.

In that short walk Trace heard a rip of gunfire off south of the tracks. It could be fun or death. A little farther on he stopped and looked back as men boiled out of a small saloon. Furious voices marked a fight. He waited for gunfire that did not come, and went on.

He had been through all this under Curby Matson in other railroad camps that had mushroomed out beyond the law. No one expected to stay after the rails moved on. Few wanted law and order. Life raced from pay day to pay day, boiling through the clamorous nights, exploding wildly on pay days.

Trace knew the answer and Curby knew it. A town like this had to he broken like a horse off the wild range, against its will, forcibly. And the town would fight back, not caring whether rails were laid or trains ran, so long as the money flowed freely.

Trace walked to the hotel that faced the tracks. He thought soberly of the five days ahead. It had to be done. The rails had to push on. He thought of the settler's wife and her grief, and strangely the thought was a help to doubts that had come as he had sat watching Susan Croston. The railroad was building for people like that now bitter wife, and others who would follow her. It was worth whatever had to be done to build. Trace doubted that Susan would understand the hard, violent reality. He knew her aunt would not.

III

The four dead men were buried the next afternoon on the swell of brown prairie north of
town, guilty and the innocent side-by-side. The
Reverend Samuel Doane, a solemn little man
with gray chin whiskers, whose church was a
weathered tent south of the railroad, stood
bareheaded beside the common grave and lifted
his voice. "Man that is born of woman . . ."

Trace stared at the common grave and thought:
The lion and the lamb shall lie down together!
His aunt used to say that. He could almost hear
her now.

An engine whistled loudly on the railroad; the
minister's words went on, and Trace looked
toward the woman who was sobbing softly. He
had marked her handkerchief going repeatedly
under a heavy black veil. Two other veiled and
stylishly dressed dance-hall girls silently sided
her without visible grief. Most of the men, Trace
guessed, had come from curiosity. Hardy Wilcox
was on the other side of the grave, standing
placidly alone. Long Jack Edwards was not
present.

It was over quickly. Trace walked past Hardy
as the three women hurried toward a polished

buggy and sleek team of matched bays. "Find out who that girl is," Trace told Hardy in a low voice, and kept going toward the black gelding he had rented.

He had not put on the badge, but he was known as the killer of one of the bandits. He saw eyes following him as he reined the black horse toward the Army fort.

The flagpole and the flag were visible when the fort was still far across the prairie. The brave flag flew high in the sunlight and west wind. It represented the long arm of government; the shield of protection raised over all the blue empty distance. Turning in the saddle, Trace saw the dwindling town and black smoke from the railroad. White-sheeted supply wagons were crawling west beside the straight new scar of unfinished grade. For a musing moment he was nine again, on the St. Louis levee, with the rock bump swelling on his head, caught by the thought of freight flowing West to families who were settling on the empty land.

Trace smiled wryly and faced toward the fort. The four dead men and the lawlessness of Denton City were hard reality against past visions, against Curby Matson's troubles, against the few short days ahead.

The flag gave way to a bull-voiced sergeant yelling commands at troopers drilling on the broad, sun-baked parade ground. Trace pinned on the punctured badge before he crossed the covered verandah of post headquarters and, with some hope, asked a fresh, pink-faced adjutant for a word with the colonel.

The hope began to fade when the spit-and-polish young second lieutenant looked him over languidly and carried in the request, his voice audible through the open door. "Sir, a civilian by the name of Ballard . . ."

The crusty reply: "That fellow? Very well, Sedgerton."

Fate gave a man like Colonel Hilary Croston a smiling brown-haired daughter who could twist a man's thoughts far from his work. A lifetime in the regulars had made the colonel what he was, a man intolerant of all things outside uniform and regulations.

He sat at the desk and listened impatiently, braid and authority on his square shoulders, long rides under a cavalryman's sun stamped in the cooked leather of his face, the handsome white mustache bold above a hard mouth, and temper rising as Trace spoke calmly.

"Keep my men inside post limits? A damned impertinent suggestion, sir."

"I only suggested putting the town outside limits for a time, Colonel."

"Same thing. There's no other place for the men to go."

Trace tried again. "It's a construction town, sir,

and out of hand. Your men may get involved in something not concerning them."

"My men can take care of themselves, Mister Ballard," Croston snapped. "That's the name, isn't it?"

"It is, Colonel."

"Yes. Well, Mister Ballard, I'm due to thank you for offering your services to my sister and daughter on their trip from Kansas City, as I requested of Mister Matson."

"Not at all, sir."

"Also," the colonel said coldly, "I understand you endangered their lives with the reckless use of your gun."

"I never use a gun recklessly, Colonel. Good day, sir."

The sun-whipped parade ground seemed to quiver as the bawling sergeant wheeled fifty sweating horses and men. Good men, who would face an Indian charge without flinching and take without complaint the bitter alkali taste of desert-swollen tongues as they followed Comanche or Apache trails out over the rim of the world. Good men, but no help to law and order when they blew off the boredom of garrison routine in a wild town.

Then Trace forgot the troopers and the colonel. The two-seated buggy just ahead on officer's row had yellow tassels fringing the top, and a fine, fast-looking pair of white horses.

Susan Croston was being helped out of the buggy by a tall young man with a mane of yellow hair. Something close to excitement hit him when Susan saw him and called: "Oh, Mister Ballard!"

He was already reining to them, swinging down, certain of her companion despite the years. "A pleasure once more, Miss Croston," Trace said. Then, to her companion: "Bud Keyhoe, isn't it?"

Susan watched, smiling, as they shook hands, measuring what the years had done to each. Bud was still the taller, solid and boldly handsome.

"I'd have known you anywhere, Trace, even if Miss Croston hadn't told me you were on the same train."

"So you got the freight wagons," Trace said, chuckling. He touched his head above the ear, remembering the rock.

Bud saw the gesture and remembered, too. He grinned. "I said I'd get the wagons, didn't I?" He saw the drilled law badge and stopped smiling. "What's that badge, Trace?"

"I'm wearing it . . . for a time."

"In town?"

"Yes."

Bud pursed his lips in a soundless whistle. "Dangerous," he remarked, and shook his head. "A little luck on the train last night makes it worse," he added.

Susan looked troubled. "There'll be more danger?" she asked.

Bud said slowly: "That badge is the real trouble. Some men in Denton City don't like badges. Trace, isn't that John Darcy's badge?"

"They tell me so." Trace smiled at Susan's troubled look, and after a moment she smiled doubtfully, still sensing more than they were putting into words. Trace's question sent her quick glance to Bud.

"What happened to Wes?" Trace asked.

Bud stood smiling and parried the question. "Wes was doing all right the last I heard. I'll tell you about him when you see me in town. Ask me about it."

Trace let it stand. He didn't look back as he rode away, skirting the parade ground and on toward the railroad. He rode thoughtfully again, with a new slow crawl of nerves in his belly, as men have in rare moments when they seem to see too well into the future.

Denton City straddled the railroad, the structures which had been erected first facing wide dusty roadways on each side of the grade. The rest straggled out to the wagon camps and more distant bed grounds of cattle drives already seeking this nearest point of shipment.

Trace rode a long swing around the outer camps, placing each tent, structure, and wagon camp clearly. Now and then he stopped for idle talk. Finally he came in past freight wagons cluttered along the railroad tracks.

Curby Matson's men were swarming about the supply spurs, tent rows, and portable warehouses, where gangs of them lived. The racket of the town closed in. Even in daytime dance-hall music struck through the work sounds. Trace dismounted behind the small plank railroad station, walked around to the front, and went in.

The agent was a dour, drawling man named Meeks, who stayed at the *clicking* telegraph key for some minutes after Trace entered. Finally Meeks pushed up a green eyeshade, adjusted black cloth sleeve guards, and came to the counter with a handful of yellow slips covered with writing.

"Here they are, mister. Copies of all telegraph messages both ways for the last four days, except train orders." Meeks complained: "I got too much work now, without all this. It don't make sense to me, anyway."

"It makes sense to Matson," Trace said good-naturedly, folding the slips and putting them inside his coat as he went out.

Hardy Wilcox was standing idly at a corner of the station, his round face placid. "Saw you ride here," Hardy said. "The girl's name is Grace Higgins. She works at the Buffalo Corral. Pretty one, they say. She's taking the day off."

"Did you find out which dead man she was crying about?"

Hardy shook his head. His cold blue eyes

considered Trace. "Her boss might know," Hardy suggested.

"Why didn't you ask him?"

"I did," Hardy said. "Fellow named Martin. He told me it was none of my business."

"Where's Long Jack?"

"Still looking the town over. There was a killing in the Buffalo Corral while you were at the fort. A gambler named Kelsey shot a big Irish grade gang foreman who made some remarks about the cards."

"Where's Kelsey now?"

"Playing cards in the same place, I guess. Want me to go talk to him?" Hardy asked mildly.

"I'll see him," Trace decided. "Then we'd better have a talk."

Hardy cleared his throat. "I saw this Kelsey kill a man at Hays City. Same kind of an argument. Kelsey wears a holster under the left arm. But he's left-handed and keeps a Derringer up his left coat sleeve."

"Thanks," Trace said.

He had an idea Hardy was watching as he rode back along the street to the Buffalo Corral, which faced the railroad. The front was painted red. Sun-bleached buffalo skulls were nailed above the entrance. Two of Curby Matson's men staggered out as Trace dismounted.

When he batted his way through the swinging doors, he found this place different. Two large portable warehouses had been set together in T-shape, the second one across the back of the first, so they formed one big building. Overhead, under the high peak of the roof, brace timbers were hung with bright cloth streamers, flags, and brass lamps.

On the right a long bar ran far back; on the left were gambling games and card tables. The dance hall was at the back, extending to right and left out of sight, with closed booths around the walls and a floor clear for dancing.

Trace guessed forty or fifty men were in the place. The bullet-drilled badge on his coat was sighted and men nudged others along the bar and turned to stare. A tightness ran through the big room and among the gambling tables, until piano music in the rear sounded loud in the spreading quiet.

Trace walked to the bar. A heavy, bearded man asked: "Looking for someone, mister?"

Trace glanced at the speaker. "A man named Kelsey in here?"

A chair scraped on Trace's left, beyond range of his vision. He watched the man at the bar.

"I ain't Kelsey," the man said.

Silence came down again. Then, from behind Ballard: "I'm Kelsey, stranger. What was it you wanted?"

Kelsey had been seated at a card table, talking with another man. He was standing when Trace turned. Tall, slender, wearing good broadcloth, immaculate linen and black string tie, everything about him said gambler. His thin face didn't look worried.

Trace looked him over carefully, noting the coat open in front, revealing the shoulder holster and gun Hardy had mentioned. Kelsey's right hand came up carelessly to the right coat lapel and Trace lost a small hope that his words would make an impression. He went to the table, stopped, and said politely: "You're leaving town, Mister Kelsey. Any direction you like. I'll walk outside with you."

"Very kind of you," Kelsey said. His right hand moved slightly. His left arm came carelessly up; he was still smiling when Trace shot the left hand into a bloody pulp.

The Derringer spinning down onto the table top told its story. Few eyes saw it. Other men were dropping to the floor or dodging to safety. Kelsey caught at the shoulder gun with his right hand and Trace shot him again.

Silence caught the big room as Kelsey fell along the table edge and down to the floor. His companion had made a crouching lunge away from the spot.

Trace wheeled, waiting for a challenge. A man stepped through the swinging doors. It was Hardy Wilcox. He looked, and turned on his heel and walked back out.

"I've taken over Darcy's job," Trace said after a moment. "When you see a badge in Denton City, do what the wearer says. Any objections?"

The bearded man, still standing in the same spot at the bar, said carefully: "Not while you've got that argument in your hand."

Trace put the gun back under his coat. "Any objections now, mister?"

"Not from me, young fellow."

A voice spoke from the back end of the long bar. "I told Kelsey he'd try that sleeve trick once too often. Have a drink on the house, gentlemen, and be friendly."

Men might say a voice could not be remembered through the long years. They were wrong. The excited prickle of old and deep memories ran through Trace as he walked toward the speaker. The young man who leaned smiling against the bar back there had dark curly hair and a cockiness about him that belonged with the memories.

"Hello, Wes," Trace said.

"Hello, Trace."

They stood eyeing each other, the past with them and no words to speak of it.

IV

"The name is Martin now," Wes said. He reached for a bar bottle and filled glasses that had been put out as Trace had started back. "Where'd you learn to shoot like that, Trace?"

"I was a green kid in the Army and a couple of mountain men taught me what they knew. I got better under Curby Matson when the U.P. was building. We had towns like this."

They had drinks and studied each other, still without words to bridge the years.

"What happened to the freight wagons you and Bud were going to have together?" Trace asked.

Wes grinned. "Bud still has some wagons. But the railroads are building fast now. A man can make money quicker other ways."

"Like this?"

"Sure."

"Why isn't Bud in it?"

Wes shrugged off the question. "That badge of Darcy's is bad luck, Trace."

"Hasn't been so far. Who killed Darcy?"

"I wouldn't tell you if I knew. Don't be a fool, Trace. Take that badge back and move on."

Trace shook his head. "Who was the man I killed on the train last night? No one seems to know him."

"I didn't go over and look at him," Wes said.

The dancing had stopped. Trace looked toward several of the girls standing about the piano. One tall blonde, he thought, had been at the graveyard with the Higgins girl. He sobered. "This is dirty business, Wes."

"There's money in it."

"Is money all you're after?"

"What else? I'm using my head," Wes said irritably. "Don't start preaching, Trace. We aren't kids any more."

Trace stood for a moment, turning the empty glass slowly in his fingers, staring at it. "We're still brothers," he said softly. "This business won't last, Wes. The town will quiet down after the railroad builds on."

"There'll be other towns," Wes said sullenly. "I know what I'm doing, and I'll keep on doing what I damned please. Don't walk in here, Trace, after all these years and start this kind of talk."

"I wonder if you ever knew what you were doing," Trace said. It was as if they were boys again. "Bud always told you what to do and you did it. How much of this business does Bud own? All of it? He used to get everything from you."

"Leave Bud out of this!"

"Was he ever out of it?"

"I told you to mind your own business," Wes said sharply. "John Darcy was the third man who didn't mind his business in this town. Use your head, Trace. Take that badge off and move on."

He was a man, speaking with sullen force, meaning it. And he was still Wes.

"I'll see you later," Trace said abruptly. He was turning away when Wes demanded: "What about Kelsey?"

"He worked for you . . . bury him," Trace said coldly, and he caught the first faint uncertainty in Wes's expression, and walked away from it, through staring silence along the bar and out the swinging doors.

Word of the shooting had passed through the town while he had talked with Wes. Mounted, Trace watched men standing alone and in little groups, eyeing John Darcy's badge and searching his face, weighing him. He was mildly surprised when he reached the hotel without trouble.

Long Jack and Hardy were waiting on a shaded bench in front. They watched silently as he tied the horse and sat down beside Long Jack.

"It's started," Trace said, taking the yellow slips from inside his coat. "Four more days. Colonel Croston won't keep his soldiers out of town."

"You see Martin?" Hardy asked.

Trace met the cold speculation in Hardy's look. "He's Wes Ballard, my kid brother. You knew it, Hardy. Something on your mind?"

"He looks like you," Hardy said. "You spoke about a brother once. Nothing on my mind, Trace."

Long Jack was leisurely using an ivory tooth-pick. He spoke past it. "Suppose we have trouble with your brother?"

Trace stared out toward the railroad track. "I'll try to see that we don't have trouble with Wes," he said, and knew it was no answer at all, and Long Jack and Hardy knew it, too, and let it hang between them.

"I haven't seen any Lazy S brands like those two horses had last night," Long Jack said past the toothpick. "The bodies we brought in don't seem familiar to anyone. At least no one will admit it."

"I looked over their guns and saddles this morning," Trace said, reading the yellow slips. "One gun had eight notches, the other three. The rest of the bunch must be as bad."

Hardy stirred restlessly. "I'm making a guess they left a trail toward the Nations, and then scattered. If they come here, I'm guessing they'll drift in from different points."

"They'll be here and we won't know it until they hit us," Long Jack said dryly.

"Curby Matson's men make more noise than trouble," Trace said. "It's the worst of the bad ones who keep the camp wild. We'll get them first . . . and quick."

"I've seen four who ought to be traveling by sundown," Long Jack remarked. "Want me to tell them?"

Trace nodded. "Put on your badge."

Hardy Wilcox silently watched Long Jack depart and slowly pinned on his own badge. "I can think of a couple myself," Hardy remarked, and, when Trace nodded, Hardy also walked away, an inoffensive-looking man.

Trace watched them go, knowing he might not see either again. He finished reading the yellow slips and put all but one back inside his coat.

The message had been sent from Kansas City to Grace Higgins, in care of Wesley Martin. It consisted of three harmless words: MOTHER LEAVING TODAY.

Trace stared at the writing, and a slow anger built deep inside as he thought of Wes. When he looked up, Bud Keyhoe was striding along the plank walk. Trace put the message in his pocket and stood up.

Bud was smiling again, big and sure of himself. "I see you've killed another one, Trace." Bud shook his head. "Better go slow. Wes says he warned you."

"How much of the Buffalo Corral do you own?" Trace asked abruptly.

Wes must have spoken of it. Bud parried the question without surprise. "Who said I owned any?"

"That's not an answer."

"It's all you'll get." Bud's smile broadened.

44

"Wes says he told you to mind your own business. Why don't you?"

Trace turned without answering as a stagecoach came from the west, the driver's long whip *cracking*.

"I own part of that line," Bud commented with satisfaction. He stepped to the edge of the walk and watched as the coach whirled gray dust toward them.

The six lathered horses pulled up sharply. Wheel brakes pressed hard. The dusty coach swerved to a stop in front of the hotel. Bud lifted a hand in greeting to the driver.

Trace looked beyond the blowing horses and wide dusty street to the rails that pointed west. "Stages won't run much longer, Bud."

"I'll have all I want by then," Bud said carelessly. "There's money where a railroad is building. There'll always be money for a man who uses his head. I'll get my share."

"You always did," Trace said.

"You never liked it, did you?" Bud asked, his smile widening, and he swung suddenly toward the sound of gunshots tearing the afternoon.

The driver dropped lightly off the front wheel and spoke dryly: "Gets woollier here every trip."

"Three shots," Bud said. He looked at Trace. "Well, Marshal?" He fell into step with Trace.

They followed hurrying men around the next

corner and found a dead man in the dust at one end of a hitch rack. Long Jack Edwards, elegant and impersonal, stood with his back against the rough board side of the building, watching faces.

"What happened?" Trace inquired.

"He's Bill Nickerson, a horse thief and killer who used to hang around El Paso," Long Jack said. "Bill saw me coming in the front door of this corner saloon with the badge on. He smelled trouble and walked out the side door there."

Keyhoe's suspicious question reached the strangers who were still gathering: "Did you follow him out and shoot him?"

Long Jack ignored him and spoke to Trace. "Bill was watching the side door there with his gun out when I went back out the front door and around the corner and called to him. Bill jumped a foot when he turned. But he came down shooting. Just a mite hasty, though."

"Did he shoot first?" Bud persisted.

"Keep out of this, Bud," Trace said curtly. Then to Long Jack: "I'll have the body moved if Nickerson doesn't have friends to claim him."

"He never had a friend," Long Jack said, and walked away.

Trace watched men stare after the tall elegant figure; the glances shifted to him, guarded, estimating. He surprised the same look on Bud's face. Puzzled. Undecided.

"I didn't know you had a deputy," Bud said.

"You know it now, Bud. Keep out of these things. You tried to put Jack Edwards in the wrong then."

Bud flushed. "What in hell do you mean?"

"Just what I said."

Bud's temper flared. His teeth showed, as when they were boys, fighting on the levee. It wiped away the years. Trace went tight, watchful. When Bud looked like that, he'd try anything. They faced each other and Bud suddenly relaxed and smiled.

"I know this town, Trace. Bill Nickerson didn't amount to much. You'd better listen to me. Go easy."

"How well did you know Nickerson?"

"He was thinking of outfitting here and going after hides this winter. We talked some."

Bud grinned again and walked away. Trace watched the man's confident carriage. He could almost feel the hard clout of farewell and hear the booming humor and warning of the bearded raftsman from the Black River country long ago: *Watch him, young' un! He'll have new tricks!*

He had a queer, disturbed feeling that nothing much had changed since that day. Nothing about Bud, Wes, or himself had changed. Only they wore guns now. Wes ran the Buffalo Corral and only a handful of days remained.

V

In the morning Trace came awake suddenly, thinking about it. About yesterday, today, tomorrow, and that telegram in care of Wes.

The stamp of yesterday was on the town when he went out for breakfast, and later walked through a tangle of freight wagons along the railroad tracks. Men watched him.

He skirted a long construction train that was loading. Shouted orders ran along the cars. Gangs of men heaved iron rails on top of other rails, and the long iron *clanged* harshly. When one looked closely, it all turned out to be orderly confusion. Some of the men gave friendly grins and Trace grinned back. Others only paused and stared.

Curby Matson came walking on one of the supply spurs. He waved as Trace cut across tracks. Matson was in fine humor, chewing the stump of the inevitable unlighted cigar when they met. "You didn't lose any time yesterday, Trace."

"It hasn't started," Trace said calmly. "You know it."

Curby rolled the cigar across his mouth and squinted against the early sunlight. "My clerk says you had more trouble at the Buffalo Corral last night."

"I asked the colonel to keep his troopers out of town. He wouldn't."

Curby was silent a moment. Then: "Did you have to shoot a sergeant? What was his name . . . Sergeant McCorkle?"

"You seem to know all about it."

"Not all," Curby denied. "I heard the sergeant was just back from a hard three weeks' patrol . . ." —Curby cleared his throat—"ready for a little fun."

"They came in town fanning lead around, and rode horses back on the dance floor at the Buffalo Corral. Four of them. You want order, Curby, or you don't. Say so now."

"It's your job," Curby admitted. "But trouble with the soldiers won't help."

"The sergeant was drunk and looking for trouble. I told him to get his horse outside and he started shooting at my feet. I couldn't get him off the horse any other way. The soldiers have got to learn, too, Curby, or the civilians won't handle. McCorkle's shoulder will be all right, if the post surgeon doesn't butcher him too much."

"Damn McCorkle and his shoulder, too! But dismounting those soldiers and sending them back to the fort in a wagon, without their guns, will have every private, non-com, and officer at the fort cursing about regimental pride."

"The colonel's opinion should be worth hearing," Trace said dryly.

Curby chuckled at the thought and changed the subject. "What about the telegrams Meeks copied? Anything in them about the payroll being on that train?"

Trace side-stepped a direct answer. "How about Meeks, Soderholm, or your clerk? Would they have talked?"

"Only Meeks and I knew," Curby said. "Meeks wouldn't talk." Curby jerked the cigar from his mouth again. "The engineer heard one man asking another if the payroll was in the car. That bunch knew! But how?"

Trace let the silence draw out. He was suddenly angry because he did. "I'll try to find out today," he promised. Something in his voice made Curby look quickly at him, start to speak, then hold silence.

In mid-afternoon, under a blue, flawless sky, with the sun thrusting hot on the far sweep of short grass, a slow, mule-drawn wagon hauled three more rough wooden boxes out on the prairie north of town. Three more. Kelsey, the gambler. Bill Nickerson, the horse thief and killer. The third a loud-boasting gunman named Brady who had overlooked the cold blue eyes in Hardy Wilcox's placid face when ordered out of town before sundown yesterday.

Hardy had watched Brady draw a gun, and had shot him once, incredibly fast, an inch above the hammered silver gun belt buckle. Hardy had walked on without comment to find his next man.

Spectators had come by dozens and scores this time, on foot and horseback, in wagons and buggies. Trace guessed half the dance-hall girls in town had come, wearing their finest clothes. The gamblers and saloon men had come, dressed in their best broadcloth and linen, some wearing high silk hats.

They were still straggling out past the smoldering chip fires of the last wagon camps when the Reverend Doane stepped to the new grave and opened his worn Bible.

Trace stood near the head of the grave, holding the reins of the black gelding—a man who seemed remote.

Wes was there, beyond the grave, alone, scowling now and then. But when Wes glanced across the newly piled dirt into Trace's unsmiling look, a faint smile jumped wryly across Wes's face, as if asking how they happened to be facing each other across this common grave outside Denton City.

Trace had been thinking it. The slow crawl of nerves came back under his belt as he looked at Wes, dressed as fine as any gambler present, handsomer than most with his dark curly hair and young, reckless look.

Bud Keyhoe had not come. Nor had many of Curby Matson's men. A few cowmen and freighters and curious travelers were in the crowd, but most of the men had soft hands and the look of easy money taken from men who worked hard.

"'I am the resurrection and the life . . .'"

Trace barely heard the solemn words. Many in the semicircle about the grave were watching him and the punctured badge John Darcy had worn. They reminded him of a wolf pack bunched and waiting.

"'Whosoever believeth in me shall never die!'"

Wes looked across the grave again, sullen, worried, and then Wes stood staring at the earth until the service was over. He was still there when the crowd began to break up. Trace turned beside the black gelding to study a lone rider far out on the prairie, heading toward town. Wes suddenly was beside him, speaking angrily.

"Don't be a fool, Trace, and turn your back on strangers. I know of two who've said they'll put lead in you when they get ready. Front or back won't matter."

"Which two men?"

Wes swore for an answer. "I could look in that hole and see you when we were kids. You were laughing like you used to, and the dirt was ready to go in on you."

A slow smile spread over Trace's face. "Did it matter?"

"Damn you," Wes said huskily. "Get out of town."

Still smiling, Trace hit him on the shoulder, gently, with a clenched fist. "Go with me?"

"I can take care of myself," Wes said.

"Can you?"

Wes cursed him again and swung away.

Trace watched him go, the smile fading. He remembered the lone rider in the distance and swung aboard the gelding and rode that way.

It was Susan Croston, riding alone.

Trace watched her easy grace in the side-saddle as she reined toward him at the gallop. The wind whipped her full skirt and streamed in the red plume curved about her small hat, and she was smiling as her blowing chestnut mare pulled up beside him. Trace pulled off his hat and turned in close beside her, smiling, too. "I wasn't sure it was you," he admitted. "Then I was afraid you'd turn back to the fort."

"I'm bringing an invitation," Susan said. She leaned forward and patted the mare's neck and gathered the reins in one small hand. "For dinner tonight, if you can come, Mister Ballard."

"Very kind of you." Trace drew a soft breath, remembering that Kelsey, the gambler, had said those same words yesterday before he died. Now dinner at the fort. The full stiffness of the colonel's quarters. The chill disapproval of Miss Agatha Croston. "I had a little trouble with the soldiers last night," Trace said, watching her.

He saw that Susan knew. Her nod was grave.

"I'm told the sergeant is in no danger now, Mister Ballard. Was it necessary to use a gun?"

"I thought so, ma'am." Still watching her, Trace added: "There was more trouble yesterday. We buried three men this morning."

"Three," Susan repeated. "Three more." She looked away, biting her lip.

"There'll be others."

"Why?"

"Ask your father the next time he sends out an armed patrol," Trace said with some bitterness, losing hope that she would understand. "This isn't Kansas City or Saint Louis."

"My father is in the Army, ordered to watch the Indians," Susan said, still not looking at him.

"Ma'am, will you look around you?" Trace asked.

Susan shifted in the side-saddle, searching his face first, and then off around the horizon, and back to him.

"What do you see?"

"I see the town and the railroad and the flag at the fort," Susan said calmly. "What should I see, Mister Ballard?"

"You'll never see it the way your eyes are looking," Trace said almost harshly. "Will you close your eyes, ma'am?"

Susan closed her eyes, flushing as she rode the slow-pacing mare in silence and waited for him to speak.

"I saw it in Saint Louis when I was boy," Trace said softly. "The settlers, ma'am. See them now if you can. The settlers heading West. Out this way. Out beyond the mountains. Women, children riding the wagons toward new homes. Thousands of them from everywhere, year after year."

Susan, her eyes still closed, answered steadily: "My father is at Fort Denton to protect them, Mister Ballard."

"They need more than protection. They need what the railroads can bring them. Some of them have been waiting a long time, ma'am. Too long."

"I know," Susan agreed. She opened her eyes, turning, studying him. "I've heard them speak of it when they visit Kansas City. The women telling of sickness and no doctors. The men complaining of high prices they must pay and low prices they get because of the long freight haul by wagons. I've heard them talk of danger, loneliness, and need of neighbors who won't come until the rail-roads are built. Isn't that what you mean, Mister Ballard?"

Trace met her level regard blankly. "You do understand," he said uncertainly. He rode for a moment, thinking of it, and then pointed toward the railroad. "Curby Matson and three thousand men are building railroad as fast as they can. They're out beyond the law." Trace stopped, not knowing exactly how to say it. "This is a hard country," he said finally. "But Curby will build his railroad. No one will interfere. Nothing else matters."

Susan gave him a long, pensive look. "My father talks of the Army as you do the railroad. Nothing else matters." Her square shoulders came back, and, after she spoke, Trace guessed she must be thinking of her aunt's tight-lipped disapproval and her father's anger over the sergeant.

"Will you come to dinner, Mister Ballard?" Susan asked.

Trace studied her and said regretfully: "I'm needed in town tonight."

The girl sobered. "You said there will be more trouble."

"I wouldn't worry about it," Trace said easily. "The railroad will be built on west and Denton City will he a quiet place before you know it."

Susan gathered the reins impatiently. "The man who wore that badge before you, Mister Ballard, must have thought the same. Are you a better judge?"

She wheeled the chestnut mare away and slashed with the quirt hanging from her wrist.

Trace reined the gelding around and watched the mare gallop toward the fort. Then he rode on toward town.

VI

He came in behind the Buffalo Corral, where small one-room plank cabins were reached by duckboard walks over the dust and mud. Trace checked the gelding and spoke to a tall auburn-haired girl who stood in a doorway, still wearing the fine silk moiré dress she had worn to the graveyard.

"Where will I find Grace Higgins, ma'am?"

She looked him over insolently. "Going to run Grace out of town, too, Marshal?"

"Maybe," Trace said. "You, too, perhaps."

She laughed. "Light and talk it over," she invited.

Trace shook his head. She shrugged. "Grace lives in Number Nine," she said.

He rode on past the numbered cabins. The auburn-haired girl walked toward the Buffalo Corral. Trace smiled thinly. She was carrying word of his presence back here at the cabins.

Number Nine was in the next row over, its solid plank door closed. The auburn-haired girl entered the back of the Buffalo Corral. Trace wondered if the Higgins girl were in there, too.

Then he saw a pink ruffled curtain stir at the cabin window. In a moment the door opened. He stepped up on the duckboards and brought off his hat to the girl who faced him.

She was a brunette with smooth olive skin and fine black hair caught at the back of her head. Her voice was bitter. "What do you want?"

Trace shook his head. "Nothing. Is there anything I can do?"

"You do for me?" Her bitterness seemed almost to touch him. "I would have had my own home. My own kitchen and furniture. Perhaps children." She swallowed hard. "I watched you bury all of it yesterday."

"What was his name?"

"Does it matter? He's dead. There'll not be another like him." Her hand touched the door frame. It was as if, inwardly, she frantically struck the rough wood. "This will be home now. Always."

"Why don't you go home to your mother?" Trace suggested.

"My mother is dead." Her lips thinned out. She searched his face and found no expression there. She said heavily: "When they bury you, I'll feel a little better."

Trace nodded. "When will they bury me?"

She straightened, looking past him toward the Buffalo Corral. Trace heard the jar of feet on the duckboards and guessed who it was. He was right. Wes was coming, a stranger striding along with him.

Trace watched the stranger. About his own age, Trace guessed, a man wearing sun-faded, wear-rumpled overalls tucked into plain boots, a stained buckskin vest, and workman-like revolvers worn low and forward. He carried a repeating rifle and walked stiff-muscled, with a tired slump to the shoulders, as if he'd not rested recently. But the long, full-lipped face had the fresh look of a barber's hand. Just in town, Trace decided, the trail stubble shaved off, and still too busy to sleep.

Wes came with an angry challenge. "What are you doing back here?"

"Talking," Trace said mildly.

Wes looked at the girl. She said: "He was asking questions."

"What questions?" the stranger demanded.

"Just questions," Trace said. He spoke to Wes and watched the stranger. "This a friend of yours?"

Wes nodded. His anger had turned to sullenness.

"Name of Smith," the stranger volunteered. He had the same cold blue eyes that were in Hardy Wilcox's placid face and none of Wes's worry. He stood easy and tired, holding the rifle loosely, sure of himself. "I know the lady," he said in the nasal tone. "She doesn't feel like answering questions today."

"Smith," Trace repeated. "New man in town?"

"An hour ago," Smith said, watching him.

"Where from?"

"West." Smith's hard blue eyes raked up from

the badge Trace wore. "I missed the burying. They tell me the law's been busy since you took over, Marshal."

"Moderately," Trace agreed.

He stepped off the boards and swung aboard the gelding, and noticed that Wes moved forward between Smith and himself as the gelding turned away.

Trace turned into the dusty way fronting the railroad and rode slowly, studying faces and the horse brands at the hitch racks. Presently he began a methodical check of the public corrals, dismounting at each, talking with the handlers and scanning horses and brands.

He saw Hardy Wilcox come out of a small saloon. He rode to meet him, and dismounted to talk.

"Strangers in town, Hardy. Wes was with one at the Buffalo Corral. Man who calls himself Smith and has been traveling hard."

"How about your brother?" Hardy asked.

"I'll handle him," Trace said. He met Hardy's gaze. "Wes acts worried. It's coming quick now. Better let Jack know."

Hardy did not ask how Trace knew. "Going to let them start it?" he asked.

"More or less." Hardy shook his head at that and Trace added: "I've got a reason."

"It better be a good reason," Hardy said, and turned away.

Trace rode toward the station. The railroad still seethed with activity from supply spurs and warehouses to the westward horizon where black smoke drifted up from the construction trains. Beyond that far smoke the long lines of heavy, loaded wagons rolled on west with supplies for the forward gangs.

Empty freight cars stood on the main track. Trace rode over and spoke to a railroad man. "These cars going East?"

"Soon as the engine hooks on, mister."

Trace turned in the saddle, gauging the low sun in the west. Curby's gangs would soon be knocking off work. The town would quickly fill with the noisy throng that kept the nights boiling. He put the horse into a trot and dismounted behind the station.

Curby Matson and Soderholm, the gaunt paymaster, were together again in Curby's boxcar office on a side track when Trace stepped inside the doorway with a brief request. "Can you hold this next string of empties East?"

Curby spun around in his desk chair. He opened the engraved case of a thick gold repeater watch and studied the time. "It's due to leave in a few minutes, Trace. Why hold it?"

"I may need it."

Soderholm cleared his throat. "Thinking of leaving us?"

Another time Trace would have smiled at the

question. He said—"Possibly."—and let it stand.

Curby sensed a difference in him. His look narrowed. "I'll hold the train," he agreed, closing the watch. "Anything else?"

"Send some carpenters with tools over to the Buffalo Corral."

Curby started to ask why. His mouth almost framed it, and then he nodded and said: "Colonel Croston is in town. Just left here. He complained about the way his men were handled last night."

"Complained?"

"He pounded the desk," Curby said dryly. "I pounded, too. Forget him."

Trace nodded. "Hold the train," he reminded, and went out.

He had to wait for the backing engine of the freight to pass before he crossed the last tracks. Yesterday he had ridden from the station to the Buffalo Corral where Kelsey waited. He rode the same way now, angling across the wide dusty street to the bone-white buffalo skulls nailed on the red-fronted building. Today it was different. The taut somberness that Curby had noted went with him into the huge bar and gambling room.

Watchful silence struck men to his right and left as he walked through the long room. The silence drew out, as he turned to the bar and spoke to a bartender.

"Where's Wes Martin?"

The bartender, fat and wheezing, sleeves rolled

up and a damp towel forgotten in his hand, said: "I'll tell Martin you asked."

"Where is he?" Trace demanded so savagely the fat man jerked a thick thumb toward the back.

"Around the corner there in his office, Marshal."

Every eye watched him as he turned right at the rear of the long bar and skirted the edge of the dance floor.

The office was in the corner ahead, its door closed. Trace tried the knob, then knocked. He heard steps come to the door and a bolt go back. Wes opened the door an inch or so, saw who it was, and said: "I'm busy, Trace."

He was closing the door when Trace hit it with his shoulder and shoved it open. Wes jumped back and brought up a revolver.

"Get out!" Wes grated.

Trace shut the door and shot the bolt. They were alone. Wes had been counting money on a table against the wall. Small stacks of gold coins stood in neat rows beside an uncounted pile of the money.

"Business must be good," Trace remarked.

He walked to the table, picked up a stack of double eagles, and ran them from one hand to the other in a *clinking* stream. He looked at several closely, put the stack down neatly, and turned, ignoring the gun.

"Grace Higgins hasn't got a mother, Wes," he said softly. "But someone back East telegraphed that her mother was leaving. It meant the pay-roll, didn't it?"

Wes went sullen again. "Prove it."

"You're guilty as hell, Wes," Trace said slowly. "A freight train out there is starting East in a few minutes. Go out and get on it."

Wes jeered at him. "You're crazy! You think I'll let you put me out of business like this?"

"I put you in business," Trace reminded. "With the old handcart. Remember? But not this kind of business, Wes. You're through now."

"We're not kids!" Wes said violently. "I can kill you with the first shot, Trace. I mean to if you crowd me with that badge."

"We were kids," Trace said. He paused. The crawl of it worked under his belt again and his mouth was dry. "My kid brother!" he said. "Now look at you. Put up that gun."

Strain was eating at Wes, too, putting a damp sheen on his sullen young face, and, when Trace moved toward him, Wes blurted thickly: "Don't make me, Trace."

VII

"I could have had a gun on you at the door," Trace said, moving forward. He was perspiring, too, his voice going harsh. That was Wes behind the gun; Wes—with his dark curly hair and stubborn recklessness, and all the past about him and between them. "You'll lose if you do it," Trace warned. "Not even Bud Keyhoe will talk it out of your mind as long as you live."

"Leave Bud out of this!"

"He was never out of it."

Wes was backing away. He stopped against the wall. "Keep back, Trace!"

"I'm building a railroad for people who need it. Your kind is holding it up, Wes. You're tearing down. Now you're through here."

"Damn you!" Wes said hoarsely. He closed his eyes. Muscles tightened in his neck. He was sweating. Trace took a last step and batted the gun aside and it went off. The report brought Wes's eyes wide open.

Always Trace would remember that look. Wes hadn't meant to shoot. Trace chopped hard with the barrel of his own gun. To the head. Above the ear. Wes's head drove back against the wall with a *thud* and he started to sag.

Trace caught him under the arms and heaved

the dead weight up over a shoulder. He turned to the table and scooped gold coins into a coat pocket. Then, with Wes facedown over the shoulder, he unbolted the door and walked out, gun cocked in his right hand.

They were waiting. The girls, the gamblers, and men who'd been at the long bar, all crowding back to see who had died in the small office.

Trace paused, balancing his burden, eyeing them. He spoke coldly through the silence. "Finish your drinks. Get your money from the games and move out. The place is closing."

He walked toward the front under Wes's dead weight and no one tried to stop him. Long Jack Edwards stepped inside as he neared the swinging doors.

"I'm closing the place," Trace said, not stopping. "There's a bunch of money on a table in his office. Get it."

"Need me with you?" Long Jack asked.

Trace shook his head. "Carpenters are coming. Tell them to nail up the doors and windows." He pushed through the swinging doors and heard Long Jack step farther into the barroom behind him.

The setting sun was slanting crimson light and lengthening shadows as Trace started across the roadway. Men stared at him. Along the busy railroad more men stopped work to watch. East of the station Curby Matson stood beside the waiting engine of the freight train.

And behind the station Bud Keyhoe's tall figure was beside a two-horse buggy, the bold yellow hair uncovered and black hat politely in one hand. Bud swung around, staring, too. And Susan Croston and her aunt Agatha looked with frozen interest from the buggy seat.

Curby Matson started to walk back from the engine. Bud said something to the two ladies and left the buggy with long, hurried strides; he arrived a moment after Trace rolled the limp figure into an empty boxcar.

"That's Wes!" Bud exclaimed. He looked into the car, at the blood showing in Wes's dark curly hair. "Did you kill him?"

Trace threw the gold coins in against Wes and stepped back, facing Bud and the approaching Matson.

"Lock him in, Curby, and let him go East," Trace said, watching Bud. "I'm closing the Buffalo Corral."

Bud's temper exploded. "You can't close the Corral or run Wes out of town!"

"Step back, Bud, or I'll send you East with him," Trace warned. He gestured with the gun.

Temper mottled Bud's face. His lips came back off the white, strong teeth. In a flash of insight Trace saw themselves facing each other on the levee long ago, and this now was a part of it, the old fight still between them, unsettled.

Bud sucked a harsh breath: "Wes ran the Buffalo

Corral for me. It's on paper, signed, witnessed. I'm taking over now."

Trace smiled tightly. "That's what I wanted you to admit, Bud. Now answer this. All the gold money I caught Wes counting in your place is scratched slightly beside the mint date. It was done when the bank made up the payroll. Who brought that money to your saloon today? And why?"

Bud's look went dark and furious and cautious. He mastered the temper and wheeled to leave. "Ask Wes," he threw back. "I let him run the place."

Curby pushed the car door shut, fastened it, and signaled the engine. A whistle answered. Couplings *clashed* and the train moved.

Trace watched the closed car start East. "My brother," he said heavily. His face was drawn and hard as he turned. "It's started, Curby. By morning you'll know how it is."

Curby chewed slowly on a cigar in a corner of his mouth. "Want me to arm some men?"

"You'd make it worse," Trace said. "I'll handle it." He turned away, too, holstering the gun under his coat.

A crowd was gathering in front of the Buffalo Corral. Bud Keyhoe had not returned to the buggy behind the station. Trace walked there.

Miss Agatha Croston looked pale. Her thin mouth set tightly when Trace came to the buggy side, hat in hand. "You ladies should return to the fort," he told them bluntly.

Susan wore the same small hat with the curving red plume. She looked under strain as she held the reins loosely. "Did Mister Keyhoe give you my message?" she asked in a low voice.

"He didn't, ma'am."

Her aunt spoke coldly. "Small wonder! I saw Mister Keyhoe threatened with a gun!"

"Bud was close to being shot and knew it," Trace agreed.

Miss Agatha gulped; her reply was stifled. "Leave this place, Susan. We're not safe here with this man."

"I think we are," Susan replied, not looking at her aunt. She hesitated. "If Mister Keyhoe was in danger, there must have been a reason." Her eyes asked Trace to say it was so.

"There was a reason," Trace said slowly. "What was Bud to tell me?"

"The enlisted men are planning to make trouble for you tonight," Susan said, meeting his look. "The sutler's wife told me. I thought you should know."

"Planning to take over the town and run me out?"

"It sounded that way."

"Susan! I understood we drove here to meet your father!" Miss Agatha protested indignantly.

The sunset light was on Susan's face. Trace waited a moment, watching her.

"Thank you, ma'am," he said, and looked toward the Buffalo Corral.

Saloons and dance halls had emptied; by scores and hundreds a crowd was gathering at the Buffalo Corral—girls and gamblers, hide hunters, cowmen, freighters, Curby's men. . . .

"You'd better drive back to the fort now," Trace said.

Susan shook her head. "My father should be here somewhere. I'll tell him about his men."

Miss Agatha spoke with shrill nervousness. "Susan! I insist. . . ." Fright struck her thin face as a gunshot slammed hard through the sunset light and its twin roared louder. "He killed that man!" Miss Agatha cried in hysterical protest as Trace spun toward the trouble.

The crowd had evidently started to scatter an instant before the shooting. Beyond the running figures, Trace saw the swinging half doors of the Buffalo Corral, Bud Keyhoe entering and Long Jack's tall figure staggering, falling to one side of the entrance.

Long Jack was a dead man, Trace guessed instantly, and was sure of it when he recognized the faded overalls and buckskin vest on the man who stood on the other side of the entrance. The stranger who called himself Smith had a rifle in one hand and a revolver in the other hand as he looked over the scattering crowd toward the station where Trace stood.

"Drive away from here!" Trace snapped to the women.

The heavy Colt gun was in his hand again as he ran hard from the buggy across the street toward a freight wagon and the nearest building fronts.

He saw Smith jerk up the rifle and fire. The whip lash pass of the bullet was close. Then he had part of the scattering crowd between himself and Smith's aim, and thought he saw two more men, then a third, with rifles, joining Smith in front of Bud's place.

Smith poised for another shot. Trace ducked behind the freight wagon and a bullet drove into the back corner of the wagon bed. Other guns opened up, hammering the wagon wood and geysering dirt underneath.

A horse coming at full gallop drew Trace's attention. The buggy was still at the station. Colonel Croston was spurring furiously toward it. The man had never ridden toward hostiles, Trace guessed, as he did now toward daughter and sister. There was a desperate look about the colonel's haste.

A heavy gun slammed twice. Uneasy quiet followed. Trace stepped from behind the wagon. Another man was down in front of the Buffalo Corral and a last swing of the half doors showed that Smith and his friends had followed Bud Keyhoe inside.

Beyond uneasy horses at a farther hitch rack

Hardy Wilcox was swiftly reloading a sawed-off shotgun from which he must have fired two buckshot loads.

Trace ran up on the boardwalk and advanced, keeping close to the building fronts. Hardy saw him, lifted a hand, and looked quickly around for threat from other directions.

Sunset light poured softly on trampled dirt and the emptiness of the wide roadway. The crowd had scattered and vanished. Here and there heads peered from cover. In doorways men silently watched Trace pass.

Hardy closed from the other direction, keeping outside the hitch racks. He fired suddenly at the doorway of Bud's place without lifting the shotgun. Splinters erupted from the swinging doors. Hardy pushed in a fresh shell and came on without any expression on his round face.

Trace stopped at a corner of Bud's big building. Long Jack lay a few steps away, the gaudy blues and yellows of his fancy silken waistcoat bright in the crimson light. He had an elegant, calm look, even in death, and the sunlight glinted on the law badge, drilled dead center by a bullet.

Hardy stopped in the street at the other corner of the building, eyeing the swinging doors. Trace tapped the hole in his own badge and indicated Long Jack's body. Hardy spat and nodded his understanding.

Trace signaled his next move. Hardy nodded

again. Trace swung back, running past the next two buildings, turning left between structures, running toward the rear of Bud's big saloon. He wondered if he was too late.

Several muleskinners had sought safety back in here. One, with a long rawhide whip coiled over a shoulder, called sarcastically: "They running you off, Marshal?"

Trace let it stand that way. The muleskinner's voice had sounded loud. Tension, almost breathless, seemed to hug the town. Since yesterday the tension had been building. Now it waited.

His own light-running steps seemed noisy as he reached the back of Bud's place. Out front the dull blast of Hardy's shotgun shook the quiet. Big pellets slapped against the rear wall inside. A voice in there yelled in angry pain and answering shots racketed out.

The duckboard walks and small cabins were off to the right. Girls watched from doorways and a few stood in the open. The black-haired Grace Higgins was defiantly in the open. She called a bitter reminder that warned anyone listening: "Tomorrow at boothill, Marshal!"

Trace ran forward. Smith must have been standing in the back doorway of the big dance room. He lunged out in the open so fast Trace's shot missed. Smith landed crouching, long full-lipped face set hard, a Colt in each hand, the right gun firing as he came down.

Trace stopped when his first shot missed. He fired again with almost deliberate care. Smith wavered, his answering shot going wild. Trace's next shot knocked him back, both guns sagging, and, when he was on the ground, he stayed there. Trace walked forward, watching the doorway, and suddenly he was spun hard and helplessly against the building, numb with shock as another gun report beat at his hearing.

He saw stupidly that his revolver was in limp fingers down against his left leg and he was falling and couldn't stop it.

He went to the ground, knowing what was happening. He struggled and there was feeling in his right side. His right arm moved. When he looked, the cabins were there before him and Bud Keyhoe was standing at the doorway of the nearest, revolver in hand, watching him. From the ground Bud looked even taller, his hair boldly yellow in the last daylight, his strong white teeth showing in a laugh as he jeered: "You never could stop me, Trace!"

Trace found his voice; it was clogged, almost a croak. "Always got a rock, haven't you, Bud?" He rolled a little, gasping to get air in a numbed chest and he glimpsed Bud watching. More feeling was back in the right arm now. His will drove the right hand over, groping for the gun held loosely in the useless left.

Bud stood watching in a kind of fascination until

74

the right hand closed on the gun. Trace struggled around, and then plopped back against the wall.

"You're licked!" Bud yelled suddenly. Lips were off his teeth as he started forward, firing wildly. A bullet struck by Trace's head, driving dirt into his face. His own big handgun seemed heavy, the hammer slow to work as he thumbed it back. He was almost dreamy, calm, somehow certain as Bud ran toward him like a wild man.

Trace fired from his position against the wall, with the right hand, hardly aiming. It was almost as if the aiming were done for him. Bud's face seemed to dissolve in a scarlet smear. Bud went down without a sound. He struggled and got his head up a little, staring for a moment, and his face went down in the dirt and he lay still.

Trace lay motionlessly, dreamily eyeing the yellow hair and thinking, queerly enough, of the big log raftsman from the Black River woods.

It was Hardy Wilcox who burst out of the back entrance, sweeping the sawed-off shotgun warily around. Hardy called back inside: "Bring whiskey!"

Hardy satisfied himself the two men were dead and knelt by Trace, the gun and his cold glance covering the cabins. "Got 'em all, I think," Hardy said evenly. "So Keyhoe was one of them, too."

"The top one," Trace said, still dreamy. "Bud always had to be the top one." He fell silent, thinking about it.

Curby Matson, holding a rifle, brought the bottle at a run, and knelt, helping Trace sit up and get a drink down. Trace choked a little, got his breath, and said: "I called Bud's hand before his full gang drifted back into town. Knew how his mind would work. He wouldn't wait, with part of the payroll there in his saloon. I've always known Bud." Curby was examining the bloody right shoulder. "Missed your lungs, I think. No blood in your mouth. I'll have the doctor at it in a few minutes."

"The soldiers are coming in tonight to take over," Trace said, worried again.

"I doubt it," Curby differed dryly. "Colonel Croston just told me over at the station that the town is out of bounds now for everyone at the fort until order is established. His sister fainted. He thinks his daughter just missed being killed." Curby stood up and shoved a cigar in the corner of his mouth. "I'd better take the colonel a drink and tell his daughter everything is all right and she can drive back to the fort now."

Trace looked up. After a moment he nodded. "Tell her it's all right now," he said.

Spawn of the Gun Pack

Marguerite E. Harper, T. T. Flynn's literary agent, made a deal with John Burr, editor of Street & Smith's *Western Story*, for her writers, including Flynn, Peter Dawson, and Luke Short, to contribute a number of stories for publication in the magazine on an annual basis. The short novels were to be approximately 20,000 words, and in 1940 T. T. Flynn didn't always give titles to the stories included in this deal, leaving this up to the magazine. This story was completed on November 1, 1940, was bought for $270 at 1½¢ a word, and appeared under the title "Spawn of the Gun Pack" in *Western Story* (4/19/41). For its appearance here, the title provided by the magazine has been retained.

I

Tom Brush killed his first man when he was fifteen, and his last when he was twenty—and in the years between, death missed him a dozen times only because he had been raised by Long Tom Kinnard.

Both had been Kinnards in those days—Long Tom and Young Tom—and Long Tom could roaringly, hilariously drink more mescal, steal more horses, and throw a gun faster than most men in the Brasada, the great thorny brush thicket between the Nueces and the Río Grande.

The dense chaparral thickets held wild cattle and reckless men, smuggling back and forth across the Río Grande, Mexicans who spoke little or no English, horse and cattle rustling for the border trade and the long trails north. Tight-lipped, hard-eyed men appeared and disappeared at Long Tom Kinnard's shack near Powdertown without saying much that the ears of Long Tom's young son could catch.

Other folks lived in the Brasada country, too: ranchers whose fenced pastures held branded cattle and horses; hard-riding, leather-guarded *vaqueros* who hit the thorny brush for monthly wages; storekeepers and working folks who grew taciturn and watchful when men like Long Tom Kinnard appeared.

Long Tom would roar about them in vast amusement when he was drinking the fiery mescal that had come over the Río Grande on burros when the moon was dark.

"A-workin' for us, they are, Pup! Grubbin' and ridin' and scrapin' and savin', and stealin' it legal from one another and trying to hold it from men smarter than they are! Rabbits, Pup! That's what they are! Rabbits! And as long as there's grass an' meat, there'll be rabbits to get fat an' wolves to ketch 'em!"

About that time, usually, Long Tom would lurch to his feet, laughing, brush the tousled black hair out of his eyes with a sweep of his hand, and take the pair of long-barreled six-guns off the wall hook and the oiled .44 Winchester out of the corner.

"Let's see how good a wolf you are, Pup! How sharp are them young teeth of your'n gettin'?"

Long Tom would lead the way back to the dry gully where old tin cans, pieces of board, sticks, and stones served for targets. There, cut off from curious eyes by the thickets of junco, black chaparral, high prickly pear, and *tasajillo* cactus, Long Tom would call approval, advice, and censure of his son's gun work. And now and then seize a gun and illustrate what he meant.

A fine, tall laughing man, that Long Tom Kinnard, with a great scorn for those who looked to others and the law for protection.

"Ask no favors an' trust no friends, Pup . . . an' you'll always make out," Long Tom would say. "Keep your face to them that don't like you, and your eyes on them that do, if you aim to stay top wolf."

And there was no one to say that Long Tom Kinnard might be wrong. The moody, bitter spells that sent Long Tom riding away alone for days at a time were no warning that the ways he preached were not best. And that late afternoon, when Long Tom came back from one such trip, there was no time to think.

Gunfire to the south was the first warning of trouble. The hard run of a madly ridden horse drummed on the cart road from Oro Wells and beyond toward the Río Grande. Young Tom reached the cactus hedge at the front of the house clearing just as his father's lathered horse burst around the curve in the road.

Long Tom was leaning forward, whipping with the rein ends and raking spurs. He was hatless, coatless, shirt ripped to ribbons and stained with blood from deep thorn scratches. He looked wild and desperate as he jerked the horse at full gallop through the hedge opening, and saw Young Tom standing there, open-mouthed. Long Tom's shout was harsh.

"Get a horse outta the corral, Pup!"

Long Tom came out of the saddle before the horse stopped, as he'd done a hundred times. Only now he did not light easily, with the spring of strength and life. He hit the sun-baked ground heavily and staggered until his outflung hand braced on the rough adobe house wall. With sudden fright, Young Tom realized that his father would have fallen if he hadn't found the dirt wall to brace against.

Long Tom must have sensed the thought. He was smiling as he stepped away from the wall. There was a terrible twisted humor about the smile that Young Tom never forgot.

"Never mind the horse, Pup," Long Tom said huskily. "I couldn't make it if there was time." He cocked his head. "An' there ain't time," he added in that same husky, strained voice. "Run back to the corral, Pup. Get that dun horse of your'n an' ride like the devil! Keep ridin' and don't come back!"

Long Tom gritted his teeth with effort as he stepped to the blowing, lathered horse and took the Winchester from the saddle scabbard. He moved as if movement were a great effort. The handsome, sun-browned face had a new strange pallor, as if all blood had drained from the flesh beneath.

"Pop . . . what's wrong?" Young Tom asked anxiously.

There was blood on Long Tom's side and hip, blood even on the fine-tooled saddle. And other riders were coming fast, just beyond the turn in the road.

"I trusted a man . . . an' he sold me out," Long Tom replied. He patted his side as he started for the open doorway. The hand was stained crimson as Long Tom held it out. "Look!" he said. "Don't forget! I got foolish an' trusted a man! Look what happened! Now take this an' ride like hell! You ain't hardly got time now!"

Young Tom took the long-barreled six-gun his father thrust at him. "They're gonna kill you, Pop!"

Long Tom swore. "Don't stand there arguin'. Get goin' like I told you. I'll take care of this. Go to Pedro Valesquez, at Santa Rosita. He'll look out for you until I get there. Now run! I'll be seein' you!" Long Tom laughed as he said that, lifting the crimson-stained hand in a parting gesture. He stopped just short of the doorway to see that his order was obeyed. "So long, Son," he said.

"So long, Pop," Young Tom said—and carried the six-gun out of sight around the little three-room adobe house.

The front door slammed shut a moment later. Young Tom heard his father *thump* a chair against the door and drag the table over. Crouching against the side of the house, Young Tom heard the first of the pursuit come racing around the turn in the road.

Throat tight, heart hammering, he inspected the gun. Even at fifteen he knew Long Tom was lying. There was fierce, grim threat in the drumming hoofs now almost to the house. . . .

The first riders burst into view on the other side of the cactus hedge. Brand riders—cowhands, *vaqueros*, brush poppers—with chin straps on their hats, heavy duck jackets, stout leather leggings.

The long-faced man leading them was Sully Johnson, who owned the Star and Gable brand east of Salt Creek. And riding just back of the ranchman was squat Sheriff Tim Harkness, who'd never liked Long Tom.

Others were coming, but Sully Johnson shouted in the quick dust haze raised by the hard-reined horses: "He's gettin' a fresh horse! There's that kid skunk of his'n primed with a gun to hold us back a few minutes!" Johnson spurred through the hedge opening, gun in his hand, shouting: "Throw down that gun, you young hellion! Where's your old man?"

Tom stepped away from the adobe wall. His shrill warning was almost as loud as Johnson's. "Stay outta here, you god-damn' killers! Get back there!"

A bullet from Sully Johnson's gun blasted dirt chips out of the wall into Tom's face before he finished. Johnson rode at him, shooting as he came.

There was no time to think. Tom backed away as he fired, too. And with the first shot, the sickening excitement that made his knees loose and weak seemed magically to vanish.

II

This was no different than shooting at bottles and sticks back in the gully, Tom discovered. Not much different than knocking over rabbits back in the brush. Only this was much easier. Horse and man were larger, slower, than a rabbit streaking from cover to cover. The gun aimed without effort, and the second crashing shot doubled Sully Johnson in the saddle.

The horse swerved sharply and Johnson pitched off, clawing futilely at the air. The rancher landed hard on the sun-baked ground, rolled loosely, like a straw-filled dummy, and stopped with his face in the dirt. Tom stared open-mouthed for a frozen moment. Johnson's legs and arms quivered, jerked, like the last shudders of a dying rabbit.

It had happened so fast that other men had not followed Johnson. Now Tim Harkness, the sheriff, yelled: "He kilt Johnson! Get him!"

And it was Long Tom Kinnard's voice that answered the sheriff. Long Tom's voice out in the open once more, roaring defiance: "Come an' get me! Let the kid alone!"

Guns opened up as Long Tom ran to meet them in the sun-drenched open space between the house and the cactus hedge. Winchester in one hand, long-barreled Colt crashing in the other hand,

Long Tom ran into the blizzard of gunfire that opened up beyond the hedge.

"Pop . . . get back!" Young Tom cried. The gunfire blotted out his voice as he started forward, sobbing, shooting, also. Horses plunged and wheeled in the hedge opening as the riders tried to fall back from Long Tom's charge. Two—three men went down. Young Tom was sure he dropped at least one.

But it was hopeless. Even at fifteen you could see that. Long Tom Kinnard had come out like a cornered wolf to defend his young. And would die for it. Was dying for it.

Long Tom stopped in mid-stride as if he had run into an invisible wall. He seemed to shake, to bow lower. His hand dropped the six-gun as he went to a knee. And then both knees. Bullets were striking dust spurts all around him.

Long Tom looked around in that moment—and his face had a hopeless smile as he saw Young Tom standing there. His arm waved the order to run.

Then Long Tom lifted the rifle and fired—and pumped in another cartridge and fired again. And then seemed to jerk and quiver and lean over quietly as if he were suddenly tired of all the fuss.

Young Tom was crying as he pulled the trigger on an empty gun. He had no more cartridges. He could give no more help to his father. No one could help Long Tom Kinnard now. And Long Tom had gestured him to run. As the first horsemen started toward him and guns opencd up at him, Tom wheeled and ran.

Lead tore his clothes in two places and was screaming closely as he ducked out of sight around the back corner of the house and raced toward the tall cactus hedge out back.

A narrow path ran back to the hidden horse corral—and those leather-guarded brush poppers could burst along it at full gallop. But at any other point the high thick hedge, bristling with fierce thorns, could stop a rider. Only a boy on foot who often went this way could pass through the small opening that had been hacked at one point.

Tom hurled himself on hands and knees through the opening as the first riders reached the back of the house. They saw him. Guns began to crash again. Bullets ripped, tore through the thorny growth.

But in a few seconds Tom was out of sight. The thorn bush beyond was almost as thick. Only a slim, stooping, dodging form could follow the almost invisible path that had been opened back into the brush. Tom had often come this way in the long hot days when there was time to kill. Sobbing, panting, he ran through the hidden paths for the last time.

Behind him the gunfire stopped. The loud angry

voices grew fainter. Riders followed the path to the corral—and the sounds they made grew fainter as Tom plunged deeper into the wilderness of thorny growth.

When he finally stopped for breath, he was alone. The cold empty six-gun was clutched in his grimy hand. He thrust it inside his braided leather pants belt and tried to swallow the raw grief that hurt his throat.

Long Tom had trusted a friend—and had died for it. The law, the ranchers, and the men who worked for the ranchers were like that. Long Tom had always said they were like that. They'd always turn on better men than themselves, when they thought they had a chance. Long Tom's crimson blood was proof!

That was the last time Tom saw the adobe house and clearing near Powdertown that had been his home since he could remember. Three days later, gaunt, crack-lipped, clothes ripped by sharp thorns, he reached the out of the way *placita* of Santa Rosita and the hut of fat Pedro Valesquez who had often come to Powdertown to see Long Tom.

"*Por diablos*, I t'ink you dead," Pedro Valesquez swore at sight of Tom, and shifted into Spanish. "We have heard. They say you were wounded and ran away. They look for you for killing the rancher, Johnson. Five hundred *pesos* reward the Johnson boy have offered to one who brings you." Pedro cleared his throat and spat. "Alive or dead, *hijo*."

Tom licked his cracked lips and said huskily: "Pop's dead, I reckon?" He touched the six-gun shoved under his belt. "I ain't got no money . . . but I got to have a horse and a few cartridges before I get on."

"Tonight," said Pedro, "you will eat an' sleep. *Mañana* there will be everything for the son of *Don* Tomás, I, Pedro Valesquez, tell you so. *Mañana* we weel cross the Río Bravo, where the son of *Don* Tomás will be safe weeth my brother Hernando. But your name you must change."

"Ain't my name good enough?"

"*Sí*, *sí*. But they have made you an outlaw, *hijo*. Eet weel spread from the Brasada. So long as you are Tomás Kinnard, you weel not be safe." Pedro shook his head regretfully. "You are too yong for that, *hijo*. What name you like?"

"Any name," Tom said, and looked down at his thorn-ripped clothes and scratched hands. The flicker of amusement that touched his drawn face had more than a hint of Long Tom Kinnard's way of laughing, had he known. "I've seen a lot of brush comin' here," he said. "How's that for a name? Tom Brush?"

"Tom . . . Tomás Brush," Pedro repeated. The fat face broke into a smile. "¡*Bueno*! My house ees yours, *Don* Tomás Brush."

So it was Tom Brush after that—and a new life

beyond the river, in old Mexico, with Hernando Valesquez, who was like sun-blackened rawhide beside his fat brother.

New ways, new faces, and sometimes an old face that had stopped at the house of Long Tom Kinnard, near Powdertown. And always action and excitement. For Hernando Valesquez and his friends dealt in contraband, back and forth across the border.

Long Tom Kinnard had directed their business on his side of the border. Long Tom's son, with a price on his head, was welcome. And when they saw the newcomer handle a six-gun, a certain grudging respect was added to the welcome. Grudging because Tom was still too young to be taken as a man.

But it was over a year before there was an answer to the questions Tom brought across the Río Grande. A year and three months—and the *cantina* in Monterrey was crowded and noisy on a *fiesta* night when Tom walked in with Hernando Valesquez and found Pete Johnson and two Brasada riders in the crowd at the bar.

This son of the man Tom had shot was swaggering and tall, and his grip on Tom's arm pressed to the bone as he sneered: "Look who's skulkin' over here in Mex country! I knowed sooner or later I'd get you, like we got that thievin' old man of yours!"

The other two Americans closed Tom in against

the bar. No guns had been drawn; the noisy crowd was paying no attention. Hernando Valesquez had vanished, which was not like the leathery little Mexican.

Tom ignored the hand on his arm. He was pale, and it was not fear. His voice shook and it was not fear, either.

"How'd you get Long Tom? Who was the dirty snake who threw him down?"

Pete Johnson was ugly, jeering; he shook Tom by the arm.

"Ain't that big talk from a feller whose maw run away. An' his paw the biggest thief in the Brasada, an' wanted by the law in Colorado."

"I'll kill you for that," Tom said huskily. "My mother died when she went East to see her folks. I've seen the letter they wrote about it. Long Tom read it to me plenty."

Pete Johnson guffawed to his grinning companions.

"His old woman took a good look at him an' his old man an' sold out from Denver with a tramp printer named Billy Baker. A cousin of ours, Buck Hayes, who knowed them all, come to visit an' seen Kinnard in Powdertown."

Tom was gulping sudden sobs and a wild new anger he'd never known. His mother had never died. Somewhere she was still alive! And Pete Johnson's grin was broad and ugly as he talked on.

" 'I'll get Kinnard for you,' Buck told my old man. 'I'll talk a buy for some wet cattle to go north, an' you can have him took on that old Colorado warrant an' anything else you ketch on him. He was crazy about that wife of his. I can handle him with talk of her.' "

Pete Johnson's guffaw and rasping words beat above the guitar music and laughter of the merry *fiesta* crowd surging into the *cantina*.

"Buck handled him, too. Pop got the sheriff an' a posse and jumped Kinnard and two more at a hide-out corral. They dropped the two men an' run Kinnard home afore they got him. An' this dirty little brush rat kilt pop!" Pete Johnson's big hand shook Tom savagely. "Now I'll settle! Come on outside, boy! Nobody'll miss you!"

One of the Brasada men had slipped Long Tom's gun from the holster at Tom's side. They hemmed him in. They were going to drag him out of the *cantina* and kill him, and, if he made a fight of it, they'd just as soon kill him in here.

Suddenly a hand came from behind, past one of the Brasada men, and thrust a knife against Tom's other hand. His fingers automatically close about it, and his husky voice cracked with wild warning as he tried to jerk loose.

"Leggo, or I'll kill you!"

Johnson cuffed him and snapped: "Grab his other arm, Brownie! Git him outta this crowd!"

And then Johnson yelled and let go as the

knife slashed across his wrist and blood spurted. Sobbing with fury, Tom jumped back against the Brasada man behind him and struck again with the knife when the man cursed and grabbed at him.

That man yelled, too, as the keen blade drove home. Yelled once and staggered to one side. A gun roared. Women started screaming. The crowd stampeded. And as Tom fought free with the naked knife blade threatening, he saw the leather-like face of Hernando Valesquez dodging from behind the second Brasada man, who was staggering forward against the bar.

Three other Mexicans, friends of Hernando, were with him. And Pete Johnson and his companions stayed there at the bar as the four Mexicans closed in behind Tom and made for the door.

They spilled out into the soft fragrant night with the stampeding crowd, and Hernando caught Tom's arm and jerked him to the left.

"Thees way, *hijo*."

Hernando led the way down a black, dusty little alley, then to the right, and through other alleys, until they reached the public corral where they had left their horses.

The other Mexicans had vanished. Hernando barked an order in Spanish for their horses, and chuckled under his breath.

"I t'ink even in Monterrey ees not good to stay now. Wen I see thees Pete Johnson weeth frien's,

I t'ink ees plenty trouble . . . so I go for help. Ees better to use knifes in crowd."

"A knife gives me the shivers," Tom said huskily. "It ain't the way to fight. But thanks, Hernando. They were goin' to settle me."

"Maybe they don' settle no one," Hernando said cheerfully. "Anyway, we leave Monterrey. Ees all right now."

"I'm leavin' for Colorado," said Tom.

"*Sí*, I t'ink so," Hernando remarked quietly. "I hear some w'at Pete Johnson say. Ees best you go. Someday quick you weel be beeg man . . . eef you live. Dangerous man because you don' trust no one moch. Hernando Valesquez weesh you luck. *Con Dios, hijo*."

III

It wasn't so easy getting to Colorado. Snow was white on the high Colorado peaks when Tom rode an old crowbait horse bareback into mushrooming Denver City. His good horse, saddle, and rifle had gone down in quicksand, and he'd barely escaped with his life and enough money to buy a skimpy outfit.

New mines were still opening up back in the mountains. New ranches, new settlers flocking in. Trying to get word of people who had lived in Denver ten years and more ago was like looking for gold back in the mountains. Nobody had ever heard of Long Tom Kinnard or a man called Buck Hayes. A half drunk printer in a newspaper shop spat tobacco juice and mumbled doubtfully: "Seems t'me when I was workin' over at Black-hawk seven, eight years ago I heered a printer say somethin' about a friend of his named Billy somebody that had bought him a press an' some paper a couple years before an' headed out Nevada way to start a paper. Don't know if his name was Baker. Never seen him myself. Nope, bud, I ain't never heard of no Buck Hayes, either. He kin of yours?"

"I aim to see him," Tom said as he left.

Winter was coming on. The high mountain

passes west were already snowing in. Tom sold the crowbait horse for $10 and searched Denver until his money was gone. Then he stole a horse from a prosperous rancher, and headed south into New Mexico. Winter would be milder down south, and a rider could get across the desert country toward Nevada.

That was the way it started, and Tom Brush kept moving. Into New Mexico Territory and Arizona Territory. Over into Nevada, where silver was like a flood and men died of thirst and hunger and hot lead, and nobody paid much attention. Millions were coming out of the ground, and more millions were waiting to be found.

There was no trace of a tramp printer named Billy Baker who had bought a wagon press and some paper, and headed out from Colorado years back. Every mining boomtown had a newspaper or two, and they moved on when the ore grew lean.

An old printer in Virginia City gave the hope that kept Tom going when he had begun to wonder if his was not a futile task. "Sure, boy, I knew Billy Baker in Denver. Billy could set type faster'n any man I ever seen. He used to talk about havin' a paper of his own to grow up with a good town. Nope, I dunno if he did or not. I heard he was seen in California a few years after that. Don't know if he had a paper or not."

A man had to live while he patiently searched.

Long Tom had taught wolf lessons well. A fast draw and a hard man behind it, even a kid, always had something to do.

The border country knew Tom Brush, and California, and down into the cattle and mining country of Chihuahua and Sonora, where *gringos* rode in off the long outlaw trails and the Yaquis killed cold-bloodedly, and the hard-riding *Rurales* kept order of a sort when they were around.

Tom hardened as he drifted, and hard men came to know the young fellow who called himself Tom Brush, and was smilingly dangerous if a stranger pressed the point. Close friends with no man, he was possessed of a wary watchfulness that saved his life more than once.

Sometimes word had already drifted ahead of the young fellow named Tom Brush, whose gun had always been quicker than the other man's gun. Before he was twenty, Tom grew used to strangers looking watchfully after they heard his name. Like the Brasada ranchmen had been toward Long Tom.

And the men his father had laughingly called rabbits were like Long Tom had said. Most of them feared a stranger who was the better man. They were fearful for their livestock, their money and possessions. They were afraid of strange guns that might challenge with smashing lead. They looked for the law to protect them. A kid with memories of Long Tom in his heart could be glad he was free, bold, and better than most men he met.

But at times something was wrong. Something that closed in when the lone campfires winked to the stars and grazing horses snorted at the clamoring coyotes. It was like a hunger that food didn't help. A lonesome restlessness that made a man moody, like those black spells that had driven Long Tom out on solitary rides through the wild thorn brush of the Brasada. A man was always alone inside, always watchful, wary.

Long Tom had been company—but Long Tom was gone. Tom Brush had a mother somewhere, but she was only a name behind Pete Johnson's sneers. A mother who'd run off from her husband and son, and maybe was dead by now. One man might know about her. The man named Buck Hayes, who'd gotten Long Tom killed, might know. But Tom was twenty before he cut Buck Hayes's trail in Mesilla, north of El Paso.

A fat bartender in a Mesilla saloon chuckled when he heard Tom's name, and said: "Tom Brush, huh? Last month you could've had a job just by walkin' in here. Good money, too."

"I've got money." Tom grinned. He spun a gold piece on the bar and poured another drink.

"Ain't a man who can't use more," the bartender said shrewdly. "And there's sure plenty of money around Red Ridge these days."

"I heard so in El Paso," Tom agreed. "They say

hell ain't half as woolly as Red Ridge these days."

"Bonanza ore. New mines still opening up. Fellow in here yesterday said they had four killings week before last. A extry good hand with a gun could do well workin' for some of the right ones. Like I said, they was talkin' in here about shooting, and a feller that knowed you said you was greased lightning with a gun. This Dave Hayes spoke up as how he'd hire a man like you for your own price."

Tom's fingers tightened on the whiskey glass. "Hayes? Dave Hayes?"

"It was Dave Hayes who said it. There's three brothers, Dave, Buck, an' Jarn Hayes. They got in early at Red Ridge and mighty near run the place now. They stick together an' own everything together, I've heard. They've got the Gold Horn Saloon, the biggest trading store, the Big Drift Mine, an' plenty of other interests."

Tom lifted his glass. His fingers were steady. He drank the whiskey and grinned as he set the glass down. "They ought to need a good man . . . as long as it's not hard-rock mining."

"Chances are it ain't mining Dave Hayes meant." The barkeep chuckled. "Them Hayes brothers'll have a job for you if you ride that way."

"I'll see them," Tom said, and the fat bartender looked slightly startled at the sudden wolfish edge to the smile he got. He was still staring uncertainly as Tom picked up his change and walked out. Out to the end of the long hunt for Buck Hayes, who had sent Long Tom Kinnard to hell with a friend's handshake and smile, and who knew the secrets of Long Tom's past.

A pack trail through the Dolorosa Mountains gave a short cut to the new boomtown of Red Ridge, above Colorado Creek, where a drifting prospector had uncovered outcropping bonanza ore. The rush that had followed had spawned Red Ridge along the creek.

The tents, blanket rolls, and wagons of the first wild rush had been quickly followed by hastily constructed huts and shacks. Then by larger frame or adobe buildings as the mines opened up. Now Red Ridge was lusty and boiling with easy money, saloons open around the clock, and the dusty streets busy day and night with miners, cowmen, gamblers, saloon girls, Mexicans, bull-team drivers, and others.

Tom Brush knew all about boomtowns. The usual crowd would be there. Most of them greedy, many hard working, many unscrupulous. And Buck Hayes would be there.

Three days later a string of heavily laden ore wagons were *creaking* out of Red Ridge to the south as Tom rode in from the Dolorosas, to the east. The wagon drivers were shouting, cursing, and *snapping* their long bullwhips with shot-like reports.

Buggies, wagons, and hitched horses lined the

dusty main street along which Tom rode, looking about him. An Indian, wrapped in a gaudy blanket despite the heat and dust, starcd impassively as Tom wrapped the reins at a rack and entered the saloon beyond. The drink he put down called for food in the small restaurant next door. Buck Hayes and his brothers could wait a little.

Two customers in the restaurant looked like cowmen. The man behind the counter had a peg-leg, a drooping red mustache, and a squint. He asked: "What'll you have, stranger?"

"Steak and potatoes, pie and coffee . . . and then some more steak."

"Steak an' spuds, you rope-headed heathen!" was called back to the kitchen. "Coffee, too. An' get another steak ready! This gent's hungry!"

A grinning Chinaman looked out of the kitchen. "Cuttee two cow. Likee red or black?"

"How you want it cooked, mister?"

"Red," Tom said. "Are those apples an' oranges to eat?"

"Two fer a dollar, mister. Your money'll give you anything from turtle soup to champagne. She's a high-rollin' town while she lasts."

One of the men near the front of the counter chuckled.

"How long'll she last, Tex, if they keep holdin' up payrolls? I hear old King Wilson ain't back yet with money to make good that last payroll he lost. They're betting him an' that high-flyin' nephew of his have been dry-gulched some-wheres down the road and dragged off outta sight."

"It'd be just my luck if they was," Tex said peevishly. "I gave two hundred dollars' worth of credit to them hard-rock men in the Wilson mine. When this payroll got took, I had to trust 'em or watch 'em eat with that fat heathen acrost the street. If old Wilson's kilt an' the pay lost again, I got to keep on trustin' 'em. Sometimes I wish I'd never heered of the grub business."

Tom grinned past the apple he was eating. "Aren't your lawmen stopping trouble any?"

Tex snorted. "Law? What law? Here comes Dave Hayes. Might be he's heard about old Wilson."

Tom bit into the apple, gauging with hard eyes the man who entered. This Dave Hayes looked like he was making money fast, and liked it. Black broadcloth trousers were tucked into fancy, expensive riding boots. A massive gold ring gleamed on a finger. A heavy gold watch chain hung across his vest. His shirt looked like silk. A cowhand's wages for two months wouldn't have bought his Stetson. The gun under his open broadcloth coat was mounted with silver and ivory.

Dave Hayes nodded at the other two customers, gave Tom a heavy-lidded stare, and sat at the counter, grunting: "Coffee."

102

"Where's that steak an' spuds?" Tex yelled back. "An' fix fresh coffee outta the Hayes can!" Tex turned back to Dave Hayes. "They heard anything about old man Wilson yet?"

Hayes bit off the end of a cigar and grinned. "Likely he went to El Paso with that nephew of his and got drunk."

"Cow come now!" the Chinaman shrilled.

Tex's pegleg *thumped* back and Tom turned to Dave Hayes.

"I heard Buck Hayes wants a good man. Where'll I find him?"

Dave Hayes stared again from the heavy-lidded eyes. "How good a man?"

"Good enough. My name's Tom Brush."

Tex was coming with the steak. The *thumping* pegleg suddenly halted. And the upjerk of Dave Hayes's head, the narrowing eyes showed that the man had heard of Tom Brush, too.

"Tom Brush?"

"That's right."

A loose-lipped smile lifted the corners of Dave Hayes's mouth. "I'll take you to Buck. He'll be leavin' in a few minutes. Tex'll keep your grub hot."

"Sure," Tex said. "Sure." His voice had a queer, strained sound.

"Suits me," Tom agreed.

Dave Hayes stood up, smiling. But something was wrong. Tom hadn't looked around, hadn't taken his eyes off Dave Hayes—but something was wrong with the sudden quiet of the restaurant man's pegleg. Something was wrong about the smile on Dave Hayes's meaty face, about his abrupt decision to see Buck Hayes. Buck Hayes had probably smiled like this before he sent Long Tom to boothill.

Dave Hayes stood there with his back to the counter, waiting for Tom to pass, and Tom stepped past the man—and looked around.

IV

All in an instant Dave Hayes had lost his smile. Already his gun was half out from under the coat. Even with that disadvantage Tom outshot him.

The bullet smashed the thick wrist and might have entered the body by the way Hayes staggered against the counter. A jump took Tom back where he could cover the two ranchmen who were about to bolt for the door. The smoking gun waved them motionless on their feet. The peg-legged restaurant man had dropped out of sight behind the counter.

"Fixing to shoot me in the back, were you?" Tom demanded.

Hayes gripped the wounded wrist with his other hand, and blood gushed out through the fingers. His look had the frozen slackness of great fear.

Tom cursed the man out of the black wrath and fury that had stayed with him since that hot afternoon long years back in the lonely Brasada.

"You dirty snake! I know your kind! I was watching for it! I'll kill you an' nobody'll miss you! Grab that gun off the floor an' use your chance!"

Beads of sweat started out on Dave Hayes's heavy face. He was pale and numb with fright. And the older of the ranchers spoke jerkily.

"How about lettin' us get out of here, young fellow? This ain't our quarrel. There'll be hell around here when the other Hayes brothers and their men start mixin' in this."

"Aren't they men enough to do it alone?"

The ranchman looked at Dave Hayes with dislike. "They've got plenty of hired guns to use. An' they'll be used. You ain't got a chance buckin' the Hayes brothers in Red Ridge. It ain't our quarrel an' we don't care to be around after the Hayes bunch hears what's happened."

"That way, is it?" Tom said. "I might 'a' known they'd work like that. Go out the back way."

The restaurant man was still out of sight behind the counter. Dave Hayes stood there in the same mute fear, blood dripping through his fingers and breath rasping through his open mouth. His eyes were on Tom's gun in horrible fascination as he waited for the shot that would kill him.

"Scared," Tom said as the two ranchers passed him on their way to the back. "By Satan, you're scared. Yellow enough to shoot a stranger in the back an' no guts when you're lookin' at his gun. Here. I'll put it up. I'll give you plenty of chance. Pick your iron off the floor an' see what you can do with a head start."

The older rancher turned at the kitchen door to see what would happen.

"I'm shot. I ain't got a chance," Dave Hayes moaned. "Don't stand there a-killin' me when I ain't got a chance. Don't kill me when I ain't got . . ."

He swayed. His mouth was still working soundlessly as he crumpled to the floor.

The rancher spoke disgustedly.

"He fainted. Dog-goned if he didn't stand there an' keel over like a woman. Better make a run for it, young fellow. You ain't got a chance if they head you off. These Hayes brothers are poison. They'll have plenty of help."

"Thanks," Tom said. "Maybe you're right. I've got more to do than get shot up by a bunch of hired gunmen."

Holstering his gun, Tom stepped out the door, where a crowd had started to gather. "Somebody help Dave Hayes! He's hurt!" Tom called at them.

And as he hoped, several men started to the door. No one tried to keep the stranger away from the hitch rack until a shout came out of the restaurant.

"Stop him! That's Tom Brush! He shot Dave Hayes!"

Tom swung into the saddle and yelled: "Look out!"

He fired twice over their heads—and in the moment of confusion he spurred down the street. Behind him guns opened up and it was easy to see what would have happened if he had been cornered in the little eating place.

Then the shots, the screaming lead cut off for a

little as Tom whirled the horse west at the first corner. But he'd be followed. Hitch racks along the street held saddled horses. Men would quickly get the other Hayes brothers into action.

Back through town to the Dolorosa trail would be heading into trouble. This way, to the west, lay a belt of brushy ridges cut by draws and dry arroyos. Tom spurred past the last shacks and corrals without looking for a road.

He was followed. A last look back before he topped the first ridge showed riders just passing the corrals. More would be coming. Dave Hayes wasn't a man to forget those paralyzing seconds he'd waited in mute fear. Tom grinned wryly as he slowed the first hard gallop that had taken him out of gunshot.

"Just my luck to get an apple and miss the steak." And he spoke to the horse: "Take it easy, boy. We aren't there yet."

The horse wasn't in shape to make too long and hard a run. Trail talk said the valley country west of Red Ridge ended at the Sobrano cliffs. Sobrano Cañon was the only way up to the higher mesas that rose to the tumbled foothills of the Cayuga range. An old wagon road went up Sobrano Cañon and swung south along the Cayuga foothills. Before the Red Ridge bonanza was discovered, the wagon road had been the only way into this country. The Sobrano lava fields were ahead, too, between Red Ridge and the cliffs.

Tom tried to think it out as he rode. That sudden trouble was queer, puzzling. In Mesilla, Buck Hayes had named a welcome for Tom Brush, had wanted the man of that name in Red Ridge for gun work to back up the Hayes brothers' poison and dirt.

And then Dave Hayes had heard the name of Tom Brush and planned cold-blooded murder in the same moment. It didn't make sense. It left questions that needed answers. And it left Buck Hayes back there in Red Ridge after the long years of searching.

But there'd be time for Tom Brush to see him; there'd be time for Tom Brush to come back and have that long overdue meeting with Buck Hayes, who had sent Long Tom to boothill, and knew all about Young Tom's mother.

The pursuit was invisible back in the brushy ridges. Tom lined a way west by the sun, past sharp, steep slopes, heavy arroyo sands, deceptive draws that tempted horse and rider off the shortest way.

The brush thinned as the ridges rolled down to flatter country. Black lava beds became visible miles ahead. And far across the lava, Sobrano Cañon looked like a slender notch in the high Sobrano cliffs.

Tom was well out on the flatter country when he sighted the pursuit and grinned with relief. They'd thought he would cut north and had angled that way. The mistake had cost them distance. More than a dozen men were in sight. The dust they raised suggested they were following the old road to Sobrano Cañon.

Tom kept straight toward the thin cañon gash in the cliffs. He'd cut across the lava beds and reach Sobrano Cañon well in the lead. The Red Ridge men were riding hard and long, but they'd probably stop at the cañon. Some of the pursuit swerved to follow him. The rest kept to the road as it swung farther away, evidently finding easy wagon passage through the lava.

The nearest riders were several miles away when Tom rode out over the first fissured lava rock. Eight or nine miles straight across, he guessed; there were new flows, older flows, and still older flows that had once pushed through here in sullen streams of smoking, crawling death.

Now the bare lava lay brown-black under the heat haze. And it didn't look far to Sobrano Cañon, where water waited and the way was clear to the mountains beyond.

Two or three miles out on the lava the black horse threw the right front shoe on the rough rock. Tom swung to get the shoe, and was sober as he rode on. A lame horse would be bad now. But the chances were they'd make it all right.

Two more miles—and Tom noticed that the lava had changed. The surface was more level and had a different look. He dismounted and looked closely. This lava was almost a rippled volcanic glass, studded with sharp points and edges. And there was no time to turn back now and hunt a way around.

Those Red Ridge riders who had followed the road might be smarter than they had seemed. They must have known about this dangerous lava. They had cut around it by the road while a few followed Tom to make sure he didn't turn back.

A mile—two miles—and there was no end to the knife-sharp edges that could chew and cut savagely at hoofs or leather shoes. Out of the past Tom remembered talk from one of Long Tom's hard-eyed visitors. Two Indian rustlers had fled across bad lava like this—and had come out on the other side flogging horses that had no hoofs left.

When the black horse finally stumbled and started to limp, Tom knew the same kind of trap had closed in on him. It was characteristic that he smiled wryly as a gambler might smile when the last chips went. And as the gambler might look around before leaving the game, Tom looked up.

Scattered clouds were tumbled fleece under the high blue sky. Not far ahead now, Sobrano Cañon waited mockingly. The high blotches of green up on the rocks had become bushes and stunted trees clinging precariously. The sunlight made a black sheen ahead that was almost beauty. Terrible beauty, when you knew what those hard sharp edges were doing.

Tom looked back. Tiny points of movement were visible far back in the shimmering heat haze. He smiled again, thin-lipped, without mirth. A man on foot wouldn't stand much chance against the Hayes brothers' gunmen. And the other bunch was coming fast on the road.

The horse stumbled again, and stopped on three legs. Tom got down, looked, and swore softly as he patted the black neck. Quickly he stripped off saddle and bridle and threw them on the ground.

"Good luck," Tom said to the horse, and began to run, carrying his rifle. A bullet might have been kinder, but even on three hoofs the horse could probably get off the lava and shift for himself.

The glass-sharp lava ground at Tom's thin boot soles. Tiny brittle projections *crunched* audibly. As stiff muscles loosened, the running was a little easier. But when Tom looked back, the moving specks were nearer.

Sweat trickled down in his eyes. He was breathing in great gasps. The lava tore and shredded at the boot soles. The boots were old; the soles too thin. They didn't last. Tom crossed the last lava in plunging awkward strides that gave no help to the agony in gashed, torn feet.

He had seen men die, some fast, some slow.

None had gone to death like this, on crippled feet, running hopelessly. The Red Ridge riders must think it fear. They meant to gun Tom Brush like a range-cornered wolf, and Red Ridge would know it wasn't safe to pull a gun on one of the Hayes brothers.

Sobrano Cañon was just ahead now. Inside the narrow cañon the Hayes men could not scatter and come in from all sides. They'd have to come together, straight off the lava, bunched and bold.

Tom's bleeding feet left a red-spotted trail. His throat was raw from the great gasping breaths that kept him going. He was weak, dizzy when he reached the little cañon creek and dropped flat to drink. Then he lurched on into the curving cañon, looking for the best place to make a stand.

A man might climb one hundred feet up the sheer cañon walls. But there he'd hang against the sheer rock face, cold meat for guns below. Then, as Tom stared around him dully, the *crack* of a whip warned him that someone was ahead of him in the cañon.

V

A rider appeared in the first curve of the cañon, then four mules pulling a rocking, canvas-topped wagon. Two more riders were followed by a second wagon with lead horses tied to the back and other riders bringing up the rear.

The first rider shouted back to the others and galloped ahead. "Howdy, stranger!" he called.

"Howdy," croaked Tom. "Got a horse to sell quick?"

The man was small and wiry, past sixty and probably nearer seventy, with a seamed face that was weathered to a dark tan. White mustache and white eyebrows stood out in sharp contrast as alert eyes looked Tom over.

"What's the matter, young feller?"

"Lost my horse on the lava," Tom said thickly. "Got to have another one quick."

Two other riders were galloping to them. Tom was startled to see that the first one was a girl in riding boots, Levi's, and tanned doeskin jacket, with a silk handkerchief at her neck and a hat hanging back on her shoulders. And Dave Hayes, back there in Red Ridge, was not dressed as well as the young dandy who followed her. Cream-colored Stetson to polished hand-stitched boots, hand-tooled gun belt and holster, expensive saddle and silver-mounted bridle, would be a sight even in El Paso or Denver. The face that went with them, a handsome, haughty face, looked Tom over suspiciously while the old man was speaking sharply to the girl.

"Sue, I said to keep with the wagons! Git on back!"

"All right, Gramp."

But the girl quieted her horse and lingered, leaning forward intently as the old man spoke to Tom.

"Lost your hoss on the lava, huh? You come straight acrost in a dad-burned hurry then. Ridin' from trouble in Red Ridge, I bet. Well, I'm sorry, stranger. Them hosses ain't mine to sell er give."

"Wouldn't surprise me if there wasn't a price on him," the young man broke in.

"You'll be surprised if your hand doesn't stop inching near that gun," Tom warned him coldly.

"Keep outta this, Bud!" the old man snapped. "Git on back with Sue if you can't keep your mouth shut!"

The young dandy flushed, scowled, and moved his hand to the saddle pommel. Tom noted that the other riders had moved up beside the second wagon, and looked ready for trouble. Not much hope now of taking a horse away from them. A surprise ambush might have done it, but the chance had passed.

The old man seemed to be ramrodding the two-wagon outfit. He'd probably fork over a horse and order the others quietly to avoid a bullet. Any man would—if the bullet were as certain as this bullet would be. No cantankerous oldster could leave Tom Brush afoot and as good as dead by stubbornly refusing to part with a horse.

Just then the girl caught her breath. "Gramp! His feet. He . . . he can hardly stand."

"I got eyes, Sue," the old man said curtly. "That lava's bad on a man afoot. Who's followin' you, young feller?"

"Never mind who's after me. Name a price for a horse."

And the long-barreled rifle whipped up to back the demand. Hard-eyed and bitter, Tom made it a choice for the old man and young man. Sell fast or get shot. Long Tom would have done it this way and laughed as he drew the gun.

The girl caught her breath and her cry was low, horrified, for Tom's ear alone. "No, no! Don't do that!"

"One of you climb down," Tom ordered hoarsely. "I'll pay . . . but I haven't got much time."

"He'll do it," the young dandy said thickly. "Hang it, I knew you shouldn't have let him get a chance like this."

"Shut up, Bud!" the old man snapped again. He spat. He was ignoring Tom's gun. His eyes had a shrewd, cool look.

"Boy, you're mighty scared or mighty tough.

An' beat out till you can't hardly stand. You'd fall off a hoss before you went far. I'm too old to scare with a gun. Shootin' me er Bud wouldn't get you no hoss. The men back there'd drop you before you got in the saddle. They're along with us all primed an' looking for trouble. The only reason they ain't here with us is because they've got orders to stick close to that wagon until I say different. Think it over." And, ignoring Tom, the old man turned to the girl. "Tell Clem Roberts to back trail fast as his hoss can make it. After dark he can circle back to Red Ridge. An' tell Clem and the other boys I'll do all the talkin' about this."

The girl reined around and put her horse in a run toward the wagons. Tom let her go. Weakness had come down on him like a soggy blanket. He was fighting to hold the rifle steady. His legs were trembling. The two men and their horses and the high rock walls of the cañon wavered before his eyes.

But the old man himself was the reason for Tom's hesitation. This one wasn't afraid of dying. A bullet threatened to knock him off the horse—and still he wasn't afraid. Only bluntly impatient.

"Maybe you oughta be caught an' took back," the old man continued. "But I'd give a dirty wolf his chance if his feet was gone an' he was helpless. Climb in that first wagon an' lay low. They won't get you."

"Tryin' tricks now?" Tom jeered.

"Call it that, son. You played the sorriest trick on yourself when you cut across the lava. Put that gun up an' climb in the wagon while you've got a chance."

The first *creaking* wagon was close. Even the driver held a rifle ready. One of the four men by the second wagon had started back up the cañon at a gallop. Desperate as he was, Tom could see he was cornered by the old man's stubborn refusal to be worried by threat of dying. The others could shoot him down or leave him on foot for the Red Ridge riders. Tom grinned. Those who knew him would have been warned by the smile.

"I'll take a chance, mister. The wagon'll be some cover. I haven't got any now. But I'll be ready for the first man who starts something."

"Proddy as a jughead, ain't you?" the old man said testily. "Just don't be a rattle-headed young fool with them guns. I give the word when trouble starts around my wagons."

Young Bud was sulky and angry about it. The driver of the first wagon, a raw-boned, sallow-faced man, stared suspiciously when ordered to stop, help the stranger inside, and keep his mouth shut about it.

The lumbering, *creaking* wagon moved on. Canvas was tightly laced across the back. The driver let the front canvas down, so that it was warm and dim inside, with the boxes, bales, and packages of the load. Tom used the rifle barrel to push an opening by the driver's shoulder and warned: "I'm watching."

"Watch till your eyes bug out," the driver retorted over his shoulder. "But keep that gun outta my ear if you got to have trouble. You an' old man Wilson are doing this. It ain't my business."

Tom had already guessed he had met old man Wilson, old King Wilson—who owned a Red Ridge mine, and was overdue in Red Ridge with his mine payroll. Old man Wilson and his high-flying nephew that Dave Hayes had sneered about. From the way Dave Hayes had sounded, old Wilson and the Hayes brothers weren't so friendly.

Old Wilson and Bud had dropped back to the rear wagon. Tom could hear the old man's rasping voice speaking to the other riders. And then the girl rode forward and spoke to the driver.

"Give him this. And men are coming."

The driver thrust a quart of whiskey in at Tom. His envy was dour. "Durned if I wouldn't like to trade places," he growled.

The strong liquor burned down and gave Tom new strength. He swore at the raw bite of pain as he poured whiskey on the bottom of one foot, and then the other. Right after that the Red Ridge men came, riding cautiously into the narrow cañon, rifles ready, eyes searching for cover that might be hiding a man on foot.

Through a slitted opening in the front canvas Tom saw them coming. Four men who had followed him across the lava and made it on their shod horses. And Tom's finger touched the rifle trigger as old King Wilson rode up beside the wagon mules and called a greeting.

The first of the Red Ridge men shouted back: "Where's that man who ran into the cañon here on foot?"

VI

The man who called the question was bigger than Dave Hayes, with a black mustache that made him look older. But there was a family likeness; this man wore the same kind of expensive clothes, had the same meaty look to his face.

Tom's face was hard as he looked through the slitted canvas and wondered if this one was Buck Hayes, who had helped kill Long Tom. Old King Wilson settled that question curtly.

"Well, Jarn Hayes, what dirty work are you an' your brothers up to now, running a man out this far?"

"Where's the yellow dog? He shot Dave and got out of town before we could stop him."

"Shot Dave, did he?" old Wilson drawled, and spat to one side of his horse. "Ain't that a pity. Dave dead?"

"Dave'll get well. His wrist is busted pretty bad."

"Who drawed first?"

"That don't matter. Dave aimed to turn him over to the law an' this man guessed it an' drawed on Dave. He's greased lightning with a gun."

"Then four of you to one ain't the edge you always like," old King Wilson said dryly. "Better not ride up the cañon huntin' him. Might be you'd meet a fight."

"By Jupiter, Wilson, you didn't let him have a fresh horse?"

Old man Wilson looked over his shoulder and called: "Git back there, Bud, with Sue! I'll do the talkin' here an' I'll make you sweat if you mix in this!"

No need to wonder what young Bud would like to say or signal to the Red Ridge men. Tom cocked the rifle. The wagon driver heard the metallic *click* and moved to the left edge of the seat where he could jump fast.

Old King Wilson snorted to the Red Ridge men: "Bud said enough about helpin' that feller. His feet was cut bad on the lava, and, anyway, I'd give a hoss to any man one of you Hayes brothers was after. You'll find tracks back up the cañon if you've got the nerve to foller. One man can do plenty with a gun up where it's tight for a wagon to get through."

Jarn Hayes swore and looked ugly. But in a moment he began to grin, and the grin was ugly, too.

"So you give him a horse? Figured you'd worry us by helping him get away. He tell you his name?"

"Didn't care enough to ask him."

"This'll make a story to tell in Red Ridge," Jarn Hayes said sarcastically. "Know what you did, Wilson? That was the dirty killer that you're offering a thousand reward for. That was Tom

Brush, who stole your payroll the other side of Apache Butte. He was on foot an' didn't have a chance . . . and you helped him get away."

Tom swore silently and gripped the rifle as he watched old King Wilson through the slitted canvas. $1,000 for Tom Brush! For a killing! For robbing old King Wilson himself!

Old Wilson only lounged easily in the saddle and answered calmly: "Too bad Dave wa'n't man enough to get the reward. I'll bet another hundred he never drawed a gun while this Tom Brush was lookin' at him. You want to bet?"

Jarn Hayes replied violently: "We'd've had him sure. Next time stay back at your blasted mine and don't mess things up."

A savage yank turned the horse into a gallop that led the Red Ridge men back the way they had come. Tom held the rifle ready as old man Wilson dropped back beside the wagon and called: "You heard him! Tom Brush?"

"That's the name," Tom admitted. "And if I'm worth a thousand for a killing and a hold-up, somebody's lied like blazes. I just came from El Paso."

"Which way was you lookin' when Dave Hayes drawed a gun on you?"

"The other way."

"I knowed I'd've won that bet," old Wilson said dryly through the wagon canvas. "Did Dave know you?"

"I asked him for a job an' told him my name."

"Told him your name was Tom Brush? You rode into Red Ridge an' told him that?"

"Why not? I never heard of your payroll. I stopped in a grub place run by a pegleg fellow named Tex. They were talkin' about your payroll hold-up before I spoke to Hayes. What happened?"

"I run short on cash money sudden an' sent to El Paso for payroll money. Some man knowed it was comin'. He held up the stage, killed the guard, made 'em pitch off my payroll, an' got away with it. Back from the road where the man had camped they found a bill of sale for a hoss. Tom Brush was the name on it. Friend of mine on the stage said he'd seen this Tom Brush once, an' it looked like the same young fellow, even if he couldn't see the face. I knowed that stage guard, too, so I offered a thousand for the man who kilt him."

"I'm Tom Brush, mister. I haven't had a bill of sale in two years, an' I pitched that one in a cook fire myself. Somebody laid your hold-up and killing on me. And planned to do it and leave that fake bill of sale behind. Who's this man who said the stranger looked like me?"

"Ain't no use bringin' him in it. Here comes Sue to fix your feet. We was bringin' some things for the doctor an' she opened the box."

"My feet'll get along," Tom said.

But old Wilson was already riding back to the rear wagon. Sue swung up on the slow-moving wagon a few moments later, opened the front canvas, and slipped inside with a small bundle.

"Take your shoes off," she directed.

"I'll be all right."

But she wouldn't have it that way. She was insistent. "Let me see your feet before they get worse."

Tom had to grit his teeth as he pulled off what was left of the old boots. He sat on a wooden crate, wary for outside sounds, as the girl doctored his feet. She was impersonal, hardly looking up.

"I'm not worth any more with my feet fixed up," Tom joshed her. "It's a thousand, alive or dead, isn't it?"

"I don't know what you're worth . . . alive or dead," Sue said briefly. "But you need help. That's why Gramp didn't turn you over to those men."

"Saves himself a thousand if he takes me in himself," Tom said

Sue flushed with quick anger. "Even a dog would be grateful for what he did. Bud was right. Gramp was foolish to help you. Hold your foot still!"

Tom admired her as she knelt there at his feet. Working on him when she didn't have to. When she'd seen him put a gun on them. And after she knew who he was.

Both feet were shapeless with bandage when Sue finished and left. And something fine and rare in Tom Brush's experience went out of the wagon with her. He rolled a cigarette, pushed the curtain back, and stared out at the lava the wagons were now skirting.

Jarn Hayes must have met the other men and turned them back. And sometime after dark the plodding mules would be in Red Ridge—where the law wanted Tom Brush for a robbery and killing, and Buck Hayes waited with his knowledge of the past.

For the first time in his life, Tom Brush was near to being helpless. No boots, feet near to useless for walking, horse and saddle gone. And cornered here in the wagon of a man who'd put a reward on his head.

"Wilson and the Hayes brothers don't seem to get along," Tom said to the raw-boned wagon driver.

"Wilson talks plain an' don't like skunks."

"How come he's back on this old road with his wagons if he went for payroll money?"

"Changed his mind and come around this way in case somebody else had a surprise cooked up for this payroll. Can't afford to lose this one. Them hard-rock men want their pay."

"His granddaughter along to help guard the money?"

"She'd be a better guard than some." The driver

turned on the seat. His long face showed emotion for the first time. "She ain't his granddaughter. She rightly ain't no relation at all, I guess. But some of us thinks a heap of her an' the way she's talked about."

"I meant it well."

The driver grunted and lapsed into morose silence. The sun slid to the western horizon as the wagons followed the little-used tracks between the lava and the Sobrano cliffs. And when the road turned to traverse the lava field, old King Wilson rode alongside the wagon leading the saddled palomino mare Sue had been riding.

"Brush," the old man said, "you can't go into town with us. They'd have you in an hour. Here's a saddle and a sack of grub. About ten miles ahead there's a hoss trail that'll get you up to the top of the rocks. Haven't got any boots for you, but you'll get along if you're as tough as you make out."

"What's the outfit worth?" Tom asked as the wagon stopped and let him down.

"The hoss an' saddle ain't for sale. Sue says to send 'em back if you get a chance. She thinks a lot of this little mare. Her father give it to her for a birthday present."

The wagon rolled on as Tom mounted the palomino mare, gathered the reins, and spoke bluntly: "I didn't hold up that stage . . . an' I won't forget this."

Sue was on the seat of the second wagon. The three armed guards and Bud Wilson were siding the wagon when Tom reined the mare alongside. Bud was scowling and the three guards showed no friendliness as Tom said: "Thanks, ma'am. You've done a lot for a stranger today: I'll get the horse an' saddle back to you."

"I'll be looking for her." Sue nodded.

"I'd like to gamble on it," sneered Bud Wilson. "Too bad I don't have the say about this."

Sue colored. "Bud, don't start any trouble. It's my horse."

Tom looked at Bud's handsome, scowling face. The dislike that leaped between them was mutual. But Tom grinned coldly.

"Maybe it's good you don't have the say, mister. You might have to back it up. Ma'am, *adiós* . . . and thanks again."

Sue lifted her hand. The flush was still on her face as she watched him ride away.

VII

Two days later, on the far slopes of the Cayuga range, Tom found sign for which he was searching. Another day brought him to one of the few bands of Mescalero Apaches still lurking more or less peacefully back in the mountains.

They had no welcome for the white stranger, but they were not hostile. They sent for a medicine man, with the Mexican name of Juan Cabeza, who would cure all wounds for gold or silver money.

Back there in the mountains where the lobo wolves howled at night, and deer meat was brought in daily by the hunters, Tom rested with Indian medicine of boiled herbs, leaves, and animal fat bound to the soles of his feet. Different medicine men used different things, but most of them could cure wounds fast.

The palomino mare grew sleeker on mountain grass. A little patience taught her to come when Tom whistled.

In a little over a week Tom's feet were as good as new, if tender, inside buckskin moccasins which one of the Apache women made for a silver dollar. More money bought a tough-muscled claybank and an old saddle from one of the men. The pony bore a Mexican brand. The saddle was punctured by bullets in two places and smeared with dark stains. Its former owner had undoubtedly been killed by raiding Apaches. Tom Brush didn't mind. Mexican horse and dead man's saddle would do for what lay ahead.

Buck Hayes waited in Red Ridge with his knowledge of the past and Long Tom's death marked against him. And someone had cold-bloodedly laid a stage robbery and killing on Tom Brush.

The man had known about Tom Brush and known when old King Wilson's payroll was coming. He was probably in Red Ridge now. He might be old Wilson's friend, the man who had said he recognized Tom Brush behind the gunman's covered face.

The girl named Sue was also in Red Ridge. Memory of her had stayed with Tom back in the mountains. The way she carried her head, with the hat jauntily and carelessly back on her shoulders. The touch of her hands as she cleaned and dressed his gashed, torn feet. She'd done all that for a stranger most people would have been covering with a gun. And the breath of a smile she'd given when he rode away on her horse had been almost friendly.

Long Tom had preached wariness, suspicion of stranger and friend alike, and proved it by the way he died. But Long Tom couldn't have meant a man like old King Wilson or a girl who gave her saddle and horse to a hunted stranger.

Tom rode the palomino mare most of the way to Red Ridge to save the Indian pony. He timed his arrival to evening darkness. The first man he met told him that King Wilson's Lucky North Mine was about a mile north of town, in the Devil's Notch, and Wilson lived on the road below the mine.

The Devil's Notch was a wide, dry ravine driving back into the Red Ridge. From the point where he left the road, Tom could see winking lantern lights far up the ravine at the Lucky North. The dull distant *rumble* of rock from an ore car drifted through the night. And all along the great ridge blinking lights marked other mines. The occasional *rumble* of rock, far-off shouts, and vague jumbled noises marked the ceaseless labor of men in the silver-veined rock.

The log and adobe house of old King Wilson was one hundred yards up the ravine, not far from the mine, yet handy to town. The house was dark save for a lamp burning dimly inside a curtained window. Tom rode to it, leading the palomino mare, and a woman's voice challenged: "Who is it?"

"Sue?"

"This isn't Sue. Who is it?"

"I'm looking for Wilson."

"He's asleep. Please be quiet."

Tom dismounted silently in the Indian moccasins and the woman came off the porch to him.

"When can I see him?" Tom asked.

"I don't know. He was worse today."

"Sounds like he's sick, ma'am."

In the starlight she peered at him. She had brought a gun from the porch. It looked like a shotgun. She was slender and erect, with gray in her hair, and her reply had the same note of challenge. "You're not from Red Ridge, or you'd know that Mister Wilson was shot last night. What do you want?"

"I'm looking for the girl who owns this horse. Maybe you know . . ."

"Thank heavens!" the woman said fervently. "No one ever thought Sue would see her mare again! Are you the one who . . . ?"

"I'm the one," Tom said.

"Then you must have been telling the truth, after all."

"Mostly I do," Tom assured her. "Where can I find her? And what happened to Wilson?"

"Sue is in town helping her father. Dave Hayes has sworn he'll have you killed on sight, young man. And the marshal likes to please those Hayes brothers, too. I'll tell Sue . . ."

The woman broke off, listening to the same thing Tom heard.

"Someone's riding from the mine," Tom said under his breath. "That gun looks like you're expecting trouble."

"We don't know what to expect," she said

hurriedly. "Mister Wilson was shot by a gunman called Slim Hilton, who picked a quarrel with him in town. No one knows why. Hilton claimed self-defense. He hasn't been arrested."

A snatch of song came through the night. The woman put her hand quickly on Tom's arm.

"That's Bud! He mustn't find you here!"

"I'll stay back of the house until he's gone."

"Then take Sue's mare with you. Bud will ask questions if he sees her."

"You think quick." Tom chuckled.

"I've had to think a lot, young man."

There was bitterness in her last remark, Tom thought as he led the horses behind the house. But he liked her. It took spunk to stand on guard here in the dark with a shotgun. Wilson's wife, probably, and not unnerved by the shooting that had put the old man near death. Bud Wilson was in high spirits as he rode to the house. Tom heard the woman's warning.

"Don't make so much noise! You'll wake your uncle!"

"How is he?" Bud asked.

"The doctor said sleep tonight would be a good sign. You don't need to come in the house. I'm doing all right."

Bud's good nature turned irritable. "You don't have to talk that way. I know you don't like me, Missus Kinnard. But I'll go in and out when I want to. Where's Sue?"

"She went to help her father."

"I told her to keep away from that newspaper," Bud said angrily. "There'll be trouble, and she may get hurt."

"Bud Wilson, who said there was going to be trouble?"

"Baker is looking for trouble if he publishes a special edition like he threatened," Bud said in a surly tone. "Sue better keep out of it. I'll tell her to go home."

He left at a gallop—and Tom came Indian-like around the house in the moccasins and startled the woman when he appeared beside her.

"Missus Kinnard . . . and Billy Baker from Denver," Tom said huskily. "You were Long Tom's wife, weren't you?"

"Who are you . . . talking about Long Tom?" Then she said: "Tom Brush!" And then caught his arm, stammering: "Tom . . . Tommy! Are you Tommy Kinnard?"

"I guess so," Tom gulped.

She dropped the shotgun unheeded as her arms went to him.

Tom caught her, too—this small, slim, gray-haired woman who held him fiercely, laughing, crying as she reached up to pat his cheek. Tom Brush's mother—Tom Kinnard's mother—out of the past that had never known the emotions that hit Tom hard as he held her.

"Long Tom said you were dead," he gulped.

"And when I heard different, I didn't know where to find you. Ever since Long Tom died, I've been hunting you. Here, lemme see your face."

"You had curls the last time I saw you, Tommy. And little fat pink cheeks. That's what I've remembered. . . ."

The flaring matches showed tears on both their cheeks. And smiles, too. Her hair was still more black than gray, her face not lined. *She was lovely,* Tom's heart cried. More beautiful than any woman he'd ever seen. His mother!

"It's still me." Tom grinned shakily as the matches went out. "And the best I can do."

Her arms went to him again.

"You're Long Tom again. Tall and handsome like he was when I met him. And the devil of recklessness in his smile. He took my baby . . . and himself has come back."

"Long Tom's dead, Mother."

But she knew it already, and sobered with him.

"Buck Hayes thought it was sport to tell me the first time he quarreled with Billy Baker in Red Ridge. He said you and your father both had been killed. He . . . he left me no hope."

"I came here to find Buck Hayes," Tom said slowly. "He double-crossed Long Tom and had him killed. I've been on his trail ever since. Hunting Buck Hayes and hunting you. Hayes left word in Texas that . . . that . . ." And something

135

else caught at Tom's heart. "Are . . . are you Sue Baker's mother?"

"Why, Tom . . . of course not. Sue's mother is down in Red Ridge. We went to school together. Laura Baker has been my best friend all my life. She and Billy Baker gave me a home when Long Tom vanished with you."

"My gosh," Tom said with gusty relief, "don't know why I said it. I guess I never understood why you went away."

"You knew Long Tom," his mother replied sadly. "I don't suppose he ever changed. He thought wrong about life, Tom. He thought most people were tricky and dishonest, and it was all right to take from them. I tried to change him, and I couldn't. And when I couldn't stand it any more and said so, Long Tom left and took you. And he never came back, because he knew I'd not change, and he'd lose you."

"That wasn't right," Tom said huskily.

"I wasn't strong like he wanted me to be strong. He wanted you, and he took you, like he took everything else he wanted. He loved me, but he thought I'd failed him, and turned against him. You belonged to him as well as to me, so he took you. Sometimes I've understood. Most times I've hated him for it."

"I can't hate him," Tom said painfully. "But . . . but . . ."

Her arm tightened around him.

"Don't think any differently of him, Son. I loved him, too. And you're so like him. Only . . . not all like him, are you?" She tried to see his face in the starlight, and fear came into her voice. "They say Tom Brush is an outlaw. A . . . a killer. They're wrong, aren't they? You're not like Long Tom, Son? Not trusting anyone? Wanting life the easy way? You know all that side of Long Tom was wrong, don't you?"

"Why . . ."

"I'd hate your father if he did that to you," she said pathetically. "But I know he didn't. Even King Wilson believed you didn't hold up that stage. Sue said you were only desperate because the Hayes men were trying to kill you for something you didn't do. Sue didn't know you, but she said you were calm and not afraid when you could hardly stagger on your feet. She knew you'd return her horse."

"I didn't believe she did," Tom muttered.

His mother wiped her eyes. "And to think it was my own boy. I'm glad I didn't know the danger you were in. They'll find out who robbed that stage and . . . and we'll never have any more trouble, will we?"

Tom's throat tightened again as he held her. There was a lot she didn't know that would hurt her. Tom Brush could hurt her like Long Tom had hurt her. And she had believed in Long Tom at one time—like Sue Baker had believed in

137

Tom Brush out there in Sobrano Cañon. "I'll find out who robbed the stage," Tom promised. "I'll settle this Buck Hayes and his brothers. And then we'll never have any more trouble."

"Tom, I . . . I never thought I'd be so happy again. And if Billy Baker is right, Buck Hayes and his brothers can say who robbed that stage. And who shot King Wilson."

"Does Baker know anything for sure?" Tom asked quickly.

"I don't know. But if he does, he'll print it, Tom. It's happened before in other towns. Billy prints what he thinks is right."

"And the Hayes brothers have warned him?"

"Yes."

"And he's down there tonight getting ready to print what he thinks?"

"Billy says he'll print a special edition, three days early, and scatter it from here to El Paso. King Wilson lived with us one winter in California, Tom. He got Billy to come here to Red Ridge and start a paper. And even sent him the money to buy a press and freight it in. He was like one of the family. Bud's folks were the only relatives he had, and he hadn't seen them for a long time. He sent for Bud, also, to share his luck."

"Bud seems plenty willing to share," Tom said grimly.

"Bud couldn't stand the easy money, Tom. He's

done more drinking and gambling than work, and Mister Wilson's had to cut off most of his money. Bud is friendly with the Hayes brothers, and doesn't want trouble with them."

"He's kind of sweet on Sue Baker, isn't he?"

"He'd like to be. Her father doesn't like him. Sue and Bud don't get along."

"I'll ride in and see this Billy Baker," Tom decided. "Might be I can help."

"No, Tom!" his mother pleaded with sudden panic. "They're looking for you. There might be shooting. I couldn't stand anything happening to you now."

"The Bakers helped you," Tom reminded. "And Sue helped me. An' now they're up against a wolf pack like the Hayes brothers . . . and no one to help them."

She sighed. "I know, Son. You're right. You'll have to help them if you can. But, Tom, you're so young to risk trouble with men like Buck and Jarn Hayes and the men who stay around them."

Tom kissed her and promised to be careful. He was smiling faintly, grimly as he left her. She was worrying about Tom Brush—whose wolf teeth had been sharpened early by Long Tom Kinnard.

VIII

Red Ridge saloons, dance halls, gambling spots, and business places were wide open, busy, and noisy. The town was roaring louder by night than by day. Tom racked his horse near the end of the main street and elbowed along the plank walks until he found a small frame building that housed the Red Ridge *Banner*.

Drawn window curtains showed light around the edges. More men seemed to be loitering along this stretch of the street than in other spots. Tom stopped at a two-foot space between the newspaper building and a saloon next door. No one paid any attention as he rolled a cigarette. The town was full of strangers.

A passing miner, bearded and booted, with tallow drippings on his overalls, stopped beside another miner and jerked his head at the newspaper windows.

"Anything happening tonight, Ed?"

Ed grinned. "Can't tell yet. Sounds like they're workin' inside. Buck Hayes came by a while ago an' looked, but he didn't say nothing."

The bearded man chuckled. "He said it all when the little rooster that owns the paper cornered him on the street this afternoon an' said the pen was mightier than the sword in bringin' justice to the wicked. An' from now on the *Banner*'ll show the world what the Hayes brothers are really like."

Ed spat and grinned, too. "Wish'd I'd seen it. They say Buck Hayes has passed the word he won't have no lies printed. And it looks like the *Banner*'s goin' to print something tonight."

The two men moved off. Tom dropped the cigarette he had been rolling and walked back between the two buildings, past the music and noise inside the saloon.

Back in the alley the night was quieter. A loud argument was in progress at a wagon yard and horse corral nearby. A drunk snored on the ground behind the saloon. Someone unbarred the back door of the *Banner* building. Quick steps took Tom to a crouch behind an empty packing case beyond the door.

No light came out when the door opened. Bud Wilson's low angry voice was audible.

"I wash my hands of it! If your father's got to be a fool, he'll have to take the consequences!"

Sue replied coldly: "All you said was not to antagonize Buck Hayes and his brothers."

"That's enough, isn't it?"

"No, it's not! If you cared anything for Gramp Wilson, you'd be doing something yourself. Doesn't it mean anything to you that he was deliberately shot down? And the coward who did it makes no secret of his friendship with Dave Hayes."

"I wasn't there. I didn't see it. Witnesses say that Slim Hilton didn't pull the first gun. Hilton told me himself he was only asking for work when the argument started."

"So you've been talking to him?" Sue flared. "Making friends with him like you think it's perfectly all right. I believe you're glad it happened! You'll have all the money you want if Gramp Wilson dies and leaves you the mine!"

"Talk like this doesn't get anywhere," Bud said angrily. "I've done all I can to make your father see sense. I wash my hands of it now."

He stamped off down the alley, muttering to himself. Sue waited a moment in the dark doorway, and then gasped as Tom stepped silently out from behind the crates.

"I brought back your horse," he said.

"Oh!" And then Sue said uncertainly: "Come in. I must bar the door."

"Missus Kinnard said you were here. Bud Wilson sounds like you're heading into trouble."

"I suppose so," Sue agreed as she secured the door on the inside. "You shouldn't have come here. Are . . . are your feet all right?"

"Fine."

Sue stepped to another door that showed chinks of light. "Father will want to talk to you. He's interested in that stage robbery."

"Going to write Tom Brush up in the paper?" Tom chuckled.

The girl opened the door, and the light made them blink at one another. Tonight Sue was wearing a dark-blue dress and jacket. Her hair was done up on her head. She was suddenly a grown-up lady, so lovely that Tom's heart began to thump.

They entered a low-ceilinged room crowded with a small printing press, racks of type, desks, tables, chairs, and stacks of paper everywhere.

"Tell Bud to get on about his business!" an irritable voice called at them. "He's in the way here."

"Father, this is the young man who borrowed my horse."

The man who stepped away from a rack of type and pushed up an eyeshade was short, quick, and nervous. Iron-gray hair was thinning to a bald spot on top, and his eyes were keen and penetrating.

"Tom Brush?" And when Tom nodded, Billy Baker pitched the eyeshade back on the type case and spoke briskly. "You couldn't have shown up at a better time. Tell me some more about this trouble with Dave Hayes."

"You've heard it, I guess," Tom said. "Hayes tried a sneak draw on me that wasn't fast enough. Over in Sobrano Cañon I heard Jarn Hayes say his brother was only trying to make an arrest. He was set for a killing."

"I can believe it," Billy Baker agreed. He was polishing his glasses. He put them on and looked

Tom over again. "Sue and King Wilson believe you didn't rob that stage."

"I was in El Paso when it happened. It wouldn't be hard to prove."

"You'd never get a chance to prove it, young man. Now who did rob the stage? Why was a bill of sale with your name on it left where it would be found?"

"Buck Hayes had me on his mind a little while before that."

Billy Baker listened to Tom's account of the conversation with the Mesilla saloon man and snapped his fingers.

"That fits in. The Hayes brothers were behind that robbery. I'll print it. After the gunman killed the guard, he told the driver to throw down the Wilson payroll. Only three men in Red Ridge knew what day the payroll was coming. I was one. King Wilson was one. Bud Wilson was the third." Billy Baker struck his fist into the other palm. "Bud Wilson can tell about that hold-up."

"Bud wouldn't," Sue protested. "It was his uncle's money. Almost like Bud's money."

"Bud made it his money. Part of it, anyway. King still doesn't know that Bud had cash money to gamble with for days after it happened," her father snapped. "And King wasn't giving it to him. It will hurt King if he lives and hears about it . . . but the truth must come out now when it will do the most good."

"Bud may have gotten drunk and said something unintentionally about the payroll," Sue protested again.

"A gunman doesn't come back and pay a man for drunken talk," her father said flatly.

"You won't get anywhere guessing about Bud Wilson or the Hayes brothers," Tom warned bluntly. "It'll only give the Hayes brothers an excuse to stop you."

"Young man, I don't print guesswork. Facts are what sway thinking people." Billy Baker turned. "Wake up, Jubal! You've had enough black coffee to sober anyone."

Behind the printing press a cot *creaked* as a man stood up. He stretched and groaned.

"I'm cold sober, and I wish I wasn't. I wish I was dead drunk in Yuma or Saint Louis. I was wondering how I ever got crazy enough to help start a fight with the Hayes brothers."

"Is this the man who robbed the stage?" Baker asked him.

Jubal Clark was a pudgy young man in a wrinkled brown suit. Hair tousled, eyes bloodshot, Clark looked haggard and morose as he walked around the printing press and regarded Tom glumly.

"This is Tom Brush, all right." He nodded. "Put a handkerchief on his face and he might pass for the man."

"Jubal's from Tucson," Baker explained. "He

saw you there last year. He was coming here to work for us, and was on the stage when it was robbed. Last night he got drunk, fell out the back door of the Gold Horn Saloon, and went to sleep on the ground."

"With a whole town to sleep in, I had to roost under that one back window," Clark muttered.

"The Hayes brothers have an office in the back of the Gold Horn," Baker explained. "The window was up a few inches. Jubal woke up and heard Dave Hayes telling a man there wouldn't be any trouble as long as he made sure no strangers were around when it happened."

"When what happened?" Tom asked.

"He didn't say," Clark replied glumly. "But when the fellow said it'd be too risky, Dave Hayes said the man's share of the Wilson payroll was gone and he ought to be glad of a chance for more easy money out of the old man."

"Could you spot that man's voice again?" Tom blurted.

"He doesn't have to," Billy Baker said calmly. "Jubal got up and looked."

Jubal Clark put a hand to his aching head. "I didn't have any better sense than to look and stagger here to tell about it. Mister Baker was out and the whiskey hit me again. I lay down behind the press there and didn't know anything until this morning, when Mister Baker opened up and told me old Mister Wilson had been shot last

146

night. I went back to the Gold Horn for a drink. The man who shot Wilson was in there with some of the Hayes men."

"Same man you saw through the window last night?" Tom guessed.

Jubal Clark nodded and groaned. "It must have been the liquor that made me get back here and tell it. How'd I know Mister Baker would corner Buck Hayes on the street and tell him that the *Banner* would print how stinking yellow and low-down the Hayes brothers are?"

Billy Baker adjusted his glasses. He looked smaller, more inoffensive than ever. But when he spoke, Tom sensed an inner strength in the little man that would have put bigger, tougher men to shame. "I'm not a gunfighter," Baker said quietly. "All I can fight with is my printing press. Red Ridge has its share of decent people. I can try to open their eyes and bring them together for some kind of action. I can shame them and show them what they're up against. While I have paper and ink and a press, I'll use them against men like these Hayes brothers."

Clark moistened his lips and looked at Tom. "He means it," he said. "He means to fight six-guns with paper. Buck Hayes has warned him there'll be hot lead and hell if he does. And still he's going to. And I haven't got sense enough to run away and stay healthy . . . and Sue won't stop him."

Billy Baker looked at his daughter. But only

when he spoke did Tom guess the love and pride that formed a bond between father and daughter.

"Sue understands," Billy Baker said in the same quiet voice.

Sue nodded. "I think he's right. I . . . I wouldn't have him do anything else."

"You see," said Billy Baker, "I'm proud of her."

Tom wanted to say something. Wanted to shout the cold, raw truth at them. But he'd seen enough to know the words would be wasted. All he said was: "Clark, how about a drink next door?"

"First sensible thing I've heard tonight," Jubal Clark declared.

Sue started to speak, but did not. But her look at Tom revealed a quick change in her. She let them out the back door, and her brief—"Thanks for returning the mare."—was cold and distant.

Her manner spoke louder than a torrent of words. She thought Tom Brush was getting out fast before the trouble broke. She thought he was running away, leaving them before he was dragged into it. So for a little she must have been glad to see him, must have counted him a friend who would approve of what they were doing.

When Sue barred the door behind them and her steps retreated, Tom caught Jubal Clark's arm.

"He's as good as dead now. He won't have a chance."

"He's got guts," Clark replied mournfully. "But

I hate to give up my gizzard on account of it. Let's get that whiskey. I need it."

"That was bait to get you out here where we can talk. How soon'll he print the paper?"

"Bait, huh? I might have known," Clark said disgustedly. "There ain't much to talk about. In an hour Billy will have papers printed to pass out on the street and start the fun. I saw most of what he's going to print. It'll scorch the hide on a mule. Those Hayeses will go crazy when they read it."

"How about the law?"

"Jesse Black, the marshal, is a bootlicker to Buck Hayes. He'll duck down a hole when trouble starts . . . and after it's over he won't know anything. Sheriff Mel Luckett stays at the Palo Verde courthouse and don't come around this hell hole any more than he has to. Luckett's not as bad as some folks think, but if Red Ridge wants to be a curly wolf, he leaves it up to the bunch that's running the town and the marshal they keep in office."

"Ought to be some folks around town that would like to see a clean-up started."

"Plenty of them," said Jubal Clark grimly. "But they keep their mouths shut and stay healthy."

Tom swore under his breath. He'd seen it all happen in other boomtowns—and had only laughed about it. Long Tom Kinnard believed that any bunch strong enough to ride a place had a right to sit in the saddle. Tom Brush had believed that, too—until now.

But this was different. This wasn't a bunch of strangers. This was Sue Baker and her father. This was old King Wilson who had helped a stranger out of a tight and sent him on his way safely. This was Tom Brush's mother—Tom Kinnard's mother—who owed much to Billy Baker and his family.

"What's that?" questioned Clark.

"I was cussing," Tom muttered. "Look, mister, you're skunked anyway if the Hayes brothers find out what you know. You might as well cut bait all the way with Billy Baker. Hunt up those people. Tell the ones you can trust that, if the Hayes brothers aren't stopped tonight, their boots will stay hard on Red Ridge. Tell them if they've got any guts at all, they'll be around somewhere to help Baker when he needs it."

"It'll be a waste of time," Clark said flatly.

"Try it anyway," urged Tom. "It's better than laying around drunk and waiting for the Hayes brothers to come looking for you. Tell the folks you can trust that hell's getting ready to bust loose . . . an', if they're all on hand ready to pick up the pieces, they'll have a town here they can run themselves."

"Who'll scatter hell into pieces they can pick up?" Clark countered sarcastically.

"Maybe no one," Tom confessed. "But I've seen

150

hell busted into pieces before . . . and it wasn't done with newspapers."

"You don't sound any crazier than Baker does," Clark admitted. "I'll do what I can." But as he started to leave, he added: "I'd a dang' sight rather be hog drunk and past thinking about what'll happen when Baker starts passing out his papers."

An hour left. Maybe less. Tom made sure his gun was loose in the holster and cartridges were ready in the rifle before he headed for the street again.

Red Ridge was waiting. A man who knew what was happening could see it now behind the dance music, the loud talk and laughter spilling out over the crowded plank walks into the dust haze that never settled on the street.

Gleefully, expectantly Red Ridge was waiting to see what would be printed about the Hayes brothers. Like an expectant crowd at a Chihuahua bullfight, the town was talking about what would happen before the kill.

The Gold Horn Saloon was the biggest building along the street, two stories high, built of rough-sawed green lumber, with a second-floor porch extending out over the walk. Hitch rack bars were between the square timbers supporting the upper porch. And tonight the big saloon was crowded to its gaping doorway.

A lanky cowman grinned when Tom asked him

151

what was going on. "Dave Hayes is buyin' drinks an' priming everybody for the fun."

"What fun?"

"Holy smokes, ain't you been around? They aim to close up the newspaper if she comes out tonight with any word about the Hayes boys."

"What about the marshal? Is he in his office?"

That brought another grin. "Most likely not, mister. If there ain't a light in the jail office, you can figure Jesse Black has left town on sudden business."

"How about his deputies?"

"The last deputy got killed when he served a warrant on the wrong man. Jesse Black ain't bothered to appoint another." The speaker jerked his head at the saloon doorway. "When Jesse needs help, he walks in there, swears in what men he needs, an' lets them handle it quick."

"If the Hayes brothers tell 'em to?"

"I didn't say that, stranger," was the quick denial, and the man turned away as if the subject had taken a turn not to his liking.

The low jail building, set off by itself at the all-but-deserted lower end of Main Street, was adobe in front and stout log walls in the back half. The office was lighted, and a saddled horse stood hitched in front.

Tom was smiling as he stepped silently into the jail office. A muscular man with rumpled black hair, vest open in front, and cigarette hanging from his lower lip was dealing solitaire at a plank table that served for a desk. He looked up, grunted—"Howdy."—and went on studying the cards.

"I'm looking for the marshal," Tom announced.

"I'm the marshal."

"Like to have you make an arrest."

The marshal threw out an ace and frowned at the cards. "See me in the morning. I'm riding outta town in a few minutes an' won't be back tonight."

"This'll have to be done tonight."

The marshal's heavy mouth split in a sarcastic grin. "What's the charge?"

"Murder."

"That so? Who got killed and who done it?" The lawman yawned as he turned up another card, placed it on his layout, and then turned up a deuce to top the ace he had just thrown out.

"Red seven on black eight," Tom said, pointing. "I don't rightly know the dead man's name. We'll get it later. The man who killed him is a dirty snake who calls himself Slim Hilton."

"What?"

"Didn't mean to make you jump, Marshal. Hilton was in on that robbery of the Wilson payroll. I'll make a complaint against Buck Hayes, too, for having knowledge of the job. Chances are he'll talk some after he's locked up."

The marshal's face was turning red as he

exploded: "Hanged if you ain't drunk! Get outta here or I'll have to lock you up!"

"Haven't had a drink tonight," Tom assured him. "Want me to sign complaints? I'll give a hand with the arrests if you need help."

The marshal threw down his cards and stood up.

"That's enough! You're drunk as all get out! I'll take them guns and lock you up until tomorrow. Don't give me any argument."

The marshal was the first man since the Mesilla bartender to see that wolfish smile. He made the mistake of reaching for his gun.

Tom's step closed distance between them as the Winchester muzzle jammed hard above the marshal's belt and doubled him up, gasping. Tom shoved the man back in the chair.

"You didn't leave town quick enough, Black. Hell is ready to pop and you aren't the man to handle it. Make me a deputy and fix papers for the Hayes brothers and this Slim Hilton. They'll get a fair trial if they come along peaceful."

"You're crazy, fellow! There'll be plenty to pay for this! I'll . . ."

"Swear me in fast, Marshal. The name is Tom Brush."

"Tom . . ." The marshal said that much and let the rest string off in a gulp as his eyes widened with alarm.

"Last chance," Tom warned him.

"Wait a minute! Don't be in a hurry. What's them names?"

The marshal clawed in the table drawer for papers and a pencil. His hand shook as he scrawled down the names. In a hoarse mumble he named Tom Brush a deputy.

And then he tried to be crafty as he stood up. "I'll go along and lend a hand," he offered.

"Where's your cell key?" Tom demanded brusquely.

"I . . ."

"Jump, you tinhorn fake!"

There were two cells, both empty, and, when the marshal's fumbling hand opened a cell door, Tom grinned coldly.

"Tricky enough even for the Hayeses, aren't you? Get in there and I'll see if I can bring you company."

For a moment the marshal remembered who he was and what was happening to him. His face twisted with a rush of anger.

"There'll be plenty done about this when Buck Hayes hears. . . ."

"I'll bet," Tom said, and the law in Red Ridge dropped like a beefed steer under the chopping gun barrel.

Tom unpinned the lawman's badge, took his belt and gun, locked the cell door, darkened the office in front, and locked the door as he left.

Better than a quarter of an hour was gone. Billy

Baker and Sue were working behind the drawn shades of the *Banner* office. Free drinks were putting the Main Street crowd in a proper frame of mind to enjoy any move the Hayes brothers made. And Tom Brush was unsmiling and catfooted in his moccasins as he reached the back of the Gold Horn Saloon.

IX

Jarn Hayes and two other men were in the back office of the saloon, drinking and talking. Hayes was speaking.

"Buck'll handle Baker himself. He gave that little squirt warning and he's mad. But while Buck's handling him, Slim, you and Whitey take some of the boys and clean out that blasted newspaper office. Bust up the press. Dump the type in a gunny sack and scatter it out beyond town. There'll be drunks enough to crowd in and make it a party."

"Bud Wilson says the girl's in there, too. What about her?"

"Push her out the back, if she won't run when you boys come in. Keep her away from the front. No use having her screaming around while Buck's taking care of her old man."

"She won't scream," Slim promised, grinning.

Glass *clinked* against glass as Jarn Hayes poured a drink.

"Don't hurt her," Hayes warned. "Bud Wilson's got an eye for her. No use getting him stirred up. He'll own the Lucky North quick now."

"And so will you," Slim said, grinning again.

That would be Slim Hilton, Tom thought—the gunman who'd shot old King Wilson. Tom's face was grim as he looked from the night at Slim's loose, grinning mouth. The young fellow was not much past twenty, and he had a weak, crafty, and reckless look.

Tom moved like a ghost in the moccasins as he stepped through the back doorway of the saloon. A piano, fiddle, and guitar were playing beyond doors and partitions. A girl was singing, but her voice was almost drowned out by the noisy uproar in the crowded barroom. Free drinks were turning the Gold Horn crowd into a mob that would be ripe for anything.

The lamplit back passage was empty as Tom stepped into the office with a gun in his hand and the same grin on his face that had made Marshal Black go for his gun.

"Reach!" Tom said as he came in and kicked the door shut behind him. "You, Hilton . . . want to get killed?"

Slim Hilton had pawed for his gun as he spun around. Then, seeing that he was too late, he jerked his hands up to shoulder level.

Jarn Hayes remained calm as he sat beside the open desk. He was calm enough to drain the whiskey glass he was holding before he put it down beside the quart bottle on the desk.

"Get out before you get hurt," he said contemptuously. "There's some things we don't like, even from drunks."

Tom backed to the window, pushed it down, and pulled down the window shade.

Whitey was the shorter, bowlegged man with a brace of guns and close-set, unblinking eyes that stared watchfully.

"Don't try it," Tom said to him. "I've got a warrant for Hilton and Jarn Hayes. Let's get going."

"Warrant?" Hayes exploded. "Who'n blazes are you, bringing a warrant here?"

"Deputy Brush. Hilton's arrested for murdering that stagecoach guard. Some of it sticks to you Hayeses. I'll take this Whitey along for good measure."

Hayes swore, black fury in his face. "I never heard of you! Black don't have a deputy! Where is he?"

"Waiting at the jail. I've got the papers and the badge."

"Deputy Brush?" Hilton said. "Brush . . . ?"

"That's right. Remember that bill of sale you planted?"

"Tom Brush!" blurted Hilton. His wide, loose mouth worked as he threw a quick look at Jarn Hayes. But Hayes was staring at the Indian moccasins on Tom's feet.

"I can walk," Tom assured him. "We'll go out the back way to the jail. Get going."

Hayes thrust his jaw out. "Why, we'll have you . . ."

"You've got me," Tom said. He holstered the gun. "Now's your chance. Who tries it first?"

They stared. The air was suddenly heavy with tension. The uproar from the front seeped back through the walls and beat against the silence.

Each of them had a gun, had a chance to draw now. The fastest man would come out on top. One of the three Hayes men—maybe two of them—would come out all right if they went for their guns.

"Whitey," Jarn Hayes said thickly.

The gunman spat on the floor and shook his head.

"Your brother Dave tried it, didn't he? I wasn't in on that stage robbery. Go for your gun and I'll back you up. But it's your call. He's come for you two."

"He's set to kill us," Hilton said hoarsely. "Look at him. Hayes . . ."

Jarn Hayes was sweating. He moistened his lips, looked at Tom, and at the other two men. "Might as well give him rope to hang himself. Buck and Dave will settle him as soon as they hear about this."

A flash of admiration came into Whitey's unblinking stare at Tom.

"I don't figure your game," the gunman said as Slim Hilton and Jarn Hayes led the way out of the office. "But you're dealing high cards, mister."

Outside in the night was the spot to make a break or pull a gun. None of them did. They reached the back of the jail building and went around to the front. Whitey took the marshal's keys at Tom's orders, unlocked the front door, and led the way in, lighting matches until he reached the big brass wall lamp, and lit it.

Jarn Hayes was sullen and furious.

"You could have done something then, Whitey. By Satan, I believe you meant to help him."

Whitey spat again. "Nope. Just taking his orders . . . like you. Pull a gun and I'll side you."

"Last chance before all of you shuck the guns and get locked in," Tom offered.

Slim Hilton put his gun belt on the table first. He was jumpy and uncertain, like a man teetering over death and not knowing why he didn't fall. The other two followed his example.

Marshal Black was still unconscious in the other cell when Tom locked them in.

"This leaves Buck Hayes and that yellow-bellied Dave," Tom told them through the bars. "As soon as they're locked up, Red Ridge'll have a chance to figure what it wants to do."

"You cleaning up Red Ridge?" Whitey asked.

"Trying to."

"By yourself?"

"Nope. I've got help."

"You'll sure as the devil need it," Whitey retorted. "And then some."

Tom smiled crookedly as he left the dark jail behind him again. Whitey didn't know that Sue Baker and her father were all the help Tom

161

Brush had. The little gunman would have laughed at him.

You didn't clean up towns like Red Ridge quietly this way. Slim Hilton and Jarn Hayes were locked up for a little. But that wouldn't clean up Red Ridge, wouldn't settle anything. Guns would talk and men would die before a town like this changed hands.

Tom Brush wouldn't get out of it alive. He'd known that when he left old King Wilson's cabin. Known it when he walked out back of the *Banner* office to question Jubal Clark.

Men would die—and Tom Brush would be one of them. Putting Jarn Hayes and Slim Hilton behind the jail bars was only a streak of luck.

Tom lifted his head and looked up the street. A noisy crowd was spilling out of the Gold Horn Saloon. Shrill whoops and yells came from the drunkest ones.

It was like an expected signal. Men began to pour out of other saloons and stores. Tom had strapped on an extra gun before he left the jail. He still had his rifle as he broke into a run, leaving the street for the darker alley that would bring him behind the *Banner* office.

Several men were loitering in the dark behind the newspaper office. Hayes men, Tom guessed, posted back here to keep Billy Baker from leaving by the rear door. They ignored the passing stranger who made for the narrow walkway

162

between the saloon and the low newspaper building.

On the plank walk Tom elbowed to the right. Down the street an occasional yell or whoop was still sounding. But here in front of Billy Baker's newspaper office the crowd was strangely quiet. Those who talked or laughed seemed guarded and uncertain.

A man near Tom said: "When Baker looked out, he said he was nigh ready with some papers. Buck Hayes is comin' to get one of the first, they say."

A stranger couldn't spot Hayes men and those who were not. Miners and gamblers were in the crowd—cowmen, Mexicans, saloon derelicts, and businessmen. All the types that made Red Ridge a roaring, reckless, money-mad town.

In the tight quiet something could be heard falling on the floor inside the building. Sue and her father were working in there. Without guns. Without help. Back to the building front, Tom eyed the crowd. Scores wore gun belts. Many would jump to obey when the Hayes brothers gave their orders. Then Tom tensed as he met a pair of eyes. It was the older of the two cowmen who had watched him shoot Dave Hayes.

"Here comes Buck and Dave Hayes!" someone called. "Let 'em through, boys!"

And a chain was unhooked inside the door and the door opened, and Billy Baker walked out bearing a big stack of folded newspapers. A dozen hands snatched for papers, passing them back into the crowd.

Sue was pale and composed as she stepped into the doorway and watched. Tom stepped behind her father and spoke curtly: "Take this rifle. Lock the door quick when he's back in. Where's Jubal Clark?"

"Drunk again, I suppose, thanks to you," Sue said coldly.

"If I don't get a chance," Tom said, "tell my mother this was in the cards. She's Missus Kinnard. She'll understand."

Then he had to turn his back on her. The newspapers had all been snatched away, and Baker had lifted his voice and was speaking: "There it is, men! Nothing but the truth! You won't have a town fit to live in unless you've got guts to do something about it!"

And a man at Tom's left whistled and exclaimed: "There'll be hell over this!"

Tom caught a glimpse of the front page that the man was scanning. Big black headlines screamed Billy Baker's message.

HAYES BROTHERS HELP OUTLAWS.
Murder and Theft Planned by Hayes Brothers
The *Banner* Demands Law and Order

"Let's see what the little squirt has printed in his damn' paper!" Tom Brush knew the man who had pushed through the crowd could be no one but Buck Hayes.

Buck was bigger than his two brothers, and dressed as flashily. His heavy black mustache was short, his beefy face redder. A newspaper was thrust into his hands. Dave Hayes, behind him, got a second paper.

Slim Hilton and Whitey weren't present to lead a wrecking bunch inside the building. But Sue Baker still stood in the lighted doorway, and her father was a slight, graying, defenseless figure that waited defiantly.

Tom jogged his elbow and spoke harshly under his breath. "For Pete's sake, get back in there an' lock the door. Hayes men are waiting out back, too."

Baker shrugged and stayed where he was.

The jostling crowd had opened a semicircle before the building as Buck Hayes swore loudly, threw the newspaper down, and tramped on it.

"I warned you, Baker, damn you!"

Tom threw one quick look over the crowd. Jubal Clark hadn't appeared. Every man in the mob might be a Hayes man, for all a stranger could tell. Tom pinned the marshal's bright badge on his coat and elbowed Baker aside as he moved quickly to face Buck Hayes.

"Your brother Jarn and his friend, Slim Hilton, are jailed for shooting that stage guard and old man Wilson," Tom said bleakly. "You're next,

Buck Hayes, and your brother Dave. You coming peacefully?"

The words struck out over the crowd. Blank silence fell. Buck Hayes exploded: "Who arrested Jarn? Who the devil are you?"

"The new deputy marshal. Got the warrants with me. Do your talking in court, Hayes."

Dave Hayes, right hand still bandaged, exclaimed: "Buck, he's Tom Brush!"

"And Tom Kinnard, too, you yellow dog," Tom retorted. "Your brother Buck remembers. Get those hands up! We're goin' to jail! There's law in Red Ridge now!"

The last was for the watching, listening crowd. They couldn't all be Hayes men.

The rancher who had watched Dave Hayes turn yellow in the restaurant was the one who lifted his voice: "That's what we need. Some honest law."

A yell came from back in the crowd: "Go to it, Marshal!"

Tom had an instant more to think of the sardonic twist that had put Tom Brush's guns fighting for the law. Then Buck Hayes sucked in a deep breath—and smiled.

"All right, Marshal, if that's the way you want it," he said smoothly. "We'll go to the jail and ask Jesse Black what this is all about. Let's see them warrants."

The man was smiling as though he wanted to

avert trouble. Smiling the way he probably had smiled when he had sold out Long Tom Kinnard down there in the Brasada. Tricky. Getting ready for a double-cross.

Billy Baker's sharp whisper proved it. "Jump, boy! On your right!"

X

Tom jumped, hands streaking for the holstered guns. Then he saw the reason for Baker's warning.

Bud Wilson was the man who had pushed out half a step in front of other men on the plank walk. Bud Wilson, wearing the cream Stetson, the hand-stitched boots, the hand-tooled gun belt and holster, Bud Wilson with his sulky handsome face scowling, and gun already up for the back shot that Buck Hayes had known was coming

Bud's gun crashed first. The cold strike of the bullet along Tom's side staggered him for a split second. A spectator cried out as the same bullet struck him. And Bud Wilson was frantically triggering another shot when Tom fired.

Sue and her father were out of it now. A dead man's hand was calling all bets. Tom Brush was ending in a blaze of crashing guns like Long Tom had died back there in the Brasada. And as on that far-off afternoon, Tom was cool. Bud Wilson had dealt a dead man's hand and had to play it out

The shot smashed Wilson in the chest—near the heart, by the way he caught convulsively at the spot. He was pitching forward as Tom whirled back in a crouch.

Grinning, Buck Hayes had his gun out to finish off the kill. The whirling crouch was a surprise by the way Hayes rattled the shot and missed. His bullet broke window glass behind Tom.

Buck Hayes's face muscles were still grinning—but his eyes popped with sudden terrified surprise as he faced another wolfish grin and two guns blasting. He screamed as the first shot struck him—and the scream was still tearing in his throat when the hammer strike of more lead cut him down.

Dave Hayes had bolted back into the crowd like a running rabbit. And the crowd itself had turned into a mad mob scrambling out of the line of fire, with other guns opening up as men backed away.

Lead shrilled past Tom. More glass broke in the windows behind him. A bullet struck him in the leg. He saw the broadcloth-coated gambler who had fired the shot, and dropped him out in the street.

"Get back!" Baker shouted at Tom. "They're ganging up down the walk there to get you!"

Tom had seen them—seven or eight men drawing together just beyond the adjoining saloon, yelling at one another and turning their guns at him.

They jumped for cover, and two of them fell as his crashing guns emptied at them. Tom threw down the empty guns as he hobbled back to Bud Wilson's body. No time to reload, but Bud Wilson's gun lay where its owner had dropped it, and Tom scooped it up and made a plunging dive for the street where Buck Hayes sprawled beside another gun.

Another figure, and still another ran to him as he came up kneeling beside the body.

"Get some cover, boy! We're helping you!"

It was the older rancher, hard-faced and grim as he fired in the direction of the Gold Horn Saloon. And backing him was the dour, lanky wagon driver of Sobrano Cañon. And other cowmen in chaps, Levi's, and spurred boots were coming with a rush to side them.

Tom staggered up on the bad leg. "Clean that bunch out by the saloon!" he ordered. "Keep 'em on the run!"

Blood was pouring down his leg as he led them at a hobbling run. Guns challenged them and then died away as men ran back through the saloon and ducked around the other side of the building.

Then a burst of yells down the street lifted above all the other sounds. Tom stepped to the edge of the walk to see better.

Save for hitched horses and waiting wagons, the street had magically cleared. Doorways, windows, spaces between buildings were packed with men waiting to see what would happen next.

The yelling men had turned into the street at the next corner. Twenty or thirty of them, armed, fanning out as they advanced.

Beside Tom a young cowman spoke harshly.

"That's Dave Hayes heading them! Ain't enough of us to buck that bunch!"

"Get under cover!" Tom directed. "I'll meet 'em!"

170

He was reloading rapidly as he hobbled out into the street. The leg felt like wood, split with pain, but it didn't matter now. Tom looked at the newspaper office. Light was still on behind the shattered window glass. The front door was closed and Billy Baker stood there with the rifle Tom had given Sue.

And as Tom limped out into the street, Baker ran to join him.

"Get back!" Tom called. "You can't help here!"

"I started it and I'm not hiding from it now!"

"You're a fool!" Tom said harshly. "But there isn't time to do anything about it now. Don't get in my way. Don't shoot until I start."

Billy Baker's newspapers were scattered up and down the street like great flakes of snow. The advancing men tramped them into the ground, and a dust haze was rising from the booted feet that grew in numbers as other men joined.

Dave Hayes was walking in front of them. There wasn't light enough to see his face plainly, but the white-bandaged hand was a give away. Tom finished reloading the guns and started hobbling down the middle of the street to meet the advancing men. And Billy Baker kept step with him, finger on the rifle trigger.

The discarded newspapers crackled and crumpled under their feet—and for an instant Tom had the grim, hopeless thought that law and order and all that Billy Baker had thought to bring to Red

Ridge was going down hopelessly in the dirt, like Baker's newspapers under the feet of these grimly approaching gunmen.

All shooting had stopped. Massed faces on both sides of the street were watching, waiting. Tom cocked the guns—and suddenly stopped, staring. "That's Jubal Clark siding Dave Hayes," he said hoarsely.

Billy Baker's voice rose in sudden excitement.

"There's Carl Garret, too. And Lem Boliver. Some of those men are miners. They can't be Hayes men. Look. Dave Hayes hasn't got a gun."

Jubal Clark ran out ahead of the others. His defiant shout rang along the street. "Where's the rest of them? We're set to make a fight of it if that's what they want!"

"Are those the men you went after?" Tom asked when Clark reached them, hatless, hair rumpled, but cold sober and no longer morose.

"We sent a man up to the Lucky North. Half the miners came down to help. Old man Wilson treated 'em square and they've been boiling about him getting shot like he did. Word was passed for everyone to meet around the corner on the next street and start together and stick together. Trouble began before we were all ready. Dave Hayes came running by so we grabbed him. He says you jailed his brother Jarn, killed his brother Buck, and killed Bud Wilson. That right?"

"Mostly."

Clark looked around. "Where's the rest of the Hayes men?"

Tom looked at the empty street behind them, at the silent watching faces at doorways and windows. He could hear now the armed men in the street calling to others to come out and help clean up the town. And singly and in twos and threes their numbers were growing as they advanced. A wry grin broke on Tom's face.

"Hayes men'll be hard to find from now on if you get the right marshal and hold 'em down," he said. "Here's the marshal's badge."

The advancing men reached and surrounded them. Hands slapped Tom Brush on the back; strangers jostled close to grab his hand and tell him he'd done everyone in Red Ridge a favor this night.

"Rabbits," Long Tom Kinnard would have called them—but they'd come out in the open to fight, too. And their hearty voices and smiling faces took a stranger into their friendship and put an unusual new surge of warm feeling into his heart. They were folks like his mother, Tom suddenly realized. Folks like Billy Baker and Sue and Jubal Clark, who wanted peace to work for their living. Peace and safety to work and make homes for their women.

Over the surrounding heads Tom saw Sue Baker standing in front of the newspaper office once more. Thought of what might have happened to her was a wrench inside him, and a hard hatred of men like Buck Hayes and his brothers, who had tried to endanger her.

Billy Baker spoke loudly. "Tom Brush here is the man for marshal!"

Others thought the same thing, and they shouted it. And then quieted to hear what Tom had to say.

"I need a doctor, not a marshal's badge," he told them, smiling a little because a lump had come in his throat. "And I've got a mother who doesn't like gun work. But I'll be around if I'm needed."

"How do we know you'll be around, friend?" one of the men called.

Sue was still there on the plank walk when Tom looked for her, and he smiled again despite the hurt in his leg and side. "I'm settling in Red Ridge, friend. I'll be staying close to home and working hard."

That satisfied them. They didn't know about those years in the Brasada and Long Tom Kinnard. They didn't know that Tom Brush was turning his back on those years calmly and without wariness. Even the men within earshot didn't know Tom Brush was turning his back on a lifetime and limping eagerly toward the future.

All they heard was Billy Baker saying: "Wait in the newspaper office with Sue until we get the doctor."

And Tom's eager reply as he started: "That suits me fine."

Last of the Fighting O'Days

T. T. Flynn completed the story he titled "The Last of the O'Days" on July 10th, 1934 and it was bought upon receipt by Rogers Terrill, editor of *Dime Western*, which during this brief period was being published twice a month by Popular Publications. The author was paid $500. The title was changed to "Last of the Fighting O'Days" when it appeared in *Dime Western* (10/1/34).

I

It began peaceably enough at Jack Diamond's bar, with six men playing stud, and it ended in red lances of gunfire and the groans of dying men and the tears of bereaved women.

Men crowded Jack Diamond's place that fateful night, jammed the bar two deep, and clustered about green baize-topped tables to watch the play. There was a fair-size group around the table where Darrel FitzLee, scion of the Double Loop, was shuffling the cards again, stacking his chips against the pile of Steve O'Day. Dave Cole, foreman of the Double Loop, was among the six players at that table; other Double Loop men were at the bar. Somewhere in town, too, was Johnny O'Day, Steve's younger brother. But Steve, in the heat of the play, wasn't thinking of Johnny, the dreamer, nor of his other brother Cass. He was playing, as he always did, recklessly, laughing a little, a taunting challenge glinting from his eyes as he laid down his cards and stretched out his hands for the pot. . . .

Destiny, as someone has said, often hinges on the turn of a card. He should have added that it also hinges on the quickness of a man's temper and on the speed with which that temper can be backed up. Young Darrel FitzLee had a temper, and so did Steve O'Day.

Darrel FitzLee had been drinking, as a gentleman should drink, straight whiskies, one after another, and, as a gentleman should, he carried his liquor well, sitting a little straighter, staring with increased brightness in his straight blue eyes. And if Darrel FitzLee's face was slightly flushed and his voice a trifle louder and tinged with arrogance as he played his cards, that was no more than was to be expected from one of the FitzLees.

Steve O'Day had won steadily since he sat in the game. The chips before him were stacked higher than any others at the table. He played with a quick recklessness that overshadowed even the sweeping size of Darrel FitzLee's bets. Steve had always been like that: quick, fiery, reckless.

"I'll tilt it ten," Steve said lightly.

"And ten," Darrel FitzLee answered.

Each man had an ace showing. Dane Walker, the houseman, had tossed an ace away with his cards. Every man at the table, and those standing behind the chairs, knew that either Steve O'Day or Darrel FitzLee had an ace for a hole card—or else each man was magnificently bluffing. Either one was capable of that to the bitter end.

Men gathered about the table, watching silently as stack after stack was pushed into the pot. Darrel FitzLee's hand was shaking slightly as he pushed his last stack in and pulled out a checkbook. His voice was high, arrogant. "I'll make it for any amount you name, O'Day," he sneered. "You seem to want a real game and, by God, I'll give it to you."

"I reckon not." Steve O'Day smiled as he shook his head. "You've been drinking a little too much. I'd end up by taking your shirt. I ain't a hog."

Slamming the checkbook on the table, Darrel FitzLee flared: "Are you saying I'm drunk?"

"Nope." Steve smiled. "But if you start writing big checks, it'll maybe make someone think you are. I'll call you."

Steve matched the last stack with one of his own and turned over his hole card—an ace. Steve had two aces. Counting the ace Dane Walker, the houseman, had thrown away and the one Darrel FitzLee had turned up, all four aces were in sight. Steve O'Day had not been bluffing. He had won in a few minutes of play the year's salary of two good top hands, for Darrel FitzLee had nothing that could match those two aces.

Steve started to sweep in the chips, with that unchanging slight smile still on his lips.

"Wait a minute!" Darrel FitzLee shouted.

The flush on the handsome face had turned into a mottled anger now. Darrel FitzLee turned over his hole card, slammed it down in the center of the table, and kicked back his chair and lurched to his feet.

Darrel FitzLee's hole card was an ace, too, the fifth ace showing in the game. "You're a damned cheat and a crooked card player, O'Day!" Darrel FitzLee charged loudly. "I might have looked for something like this when I sat down in a game with scum like you!"

The smile vanished from Steve O'Day's face, leaving it bleak and impassive. He spoke coldly: "My game was straight. I don't know a damn' thing about that fifth card. Calm down an' let's straighten this out."

"You're a liar," Darrel FitzLee said thickly. "And there's only one way to straighten out a crooked play." Men standing back of the chairs scattered as Darrel FitzLee reached for his holster.

"Wait a minute!" Steve O'Day yelled. "Don't do that!"

His hand was snapping to his hip as he finished speaking, for Darrel FitzLee's hand was already at his thigh, drawing his gun.

Steve O'Day got his gun out first as he came to his feet. He had been noted since a boy for his quick, deadly shooting ability. All three of the O'Day boys were crack shots.

Darrel FitzLee would not have had a chance if it hadn't been for Dave Cole. No one had paid any attention to the Double Loop foreman, whose thin pointed face and silent manner carried him through life always in the background—and the more effective and deadly for it. Now, unexpectedly, Dave Cole's big belt gun blasted over the edge of the table, blasted at Steve O'Day a bare arm's length away where no man could have missed him.

The bullet struck Steve O'Day in the chest. He staggered back a step, faltered, and, as he stood there in a half daze, Darrel FitzLee shot him again.

Steve O'Day was done for. Steve O'Day knew it. The daze passed. He spread his legs to brace his tottering body. He smiled thinly again while the swift glaze of onrushing death came over his eyes. He lifted his gun with calm, deliberate effort and shot once at Darrel FitzLee as the two other guns blasted at him again.

Yes, Steve O'Day was done for. He went down on the loose sawdust that covered the floor, landing heavily, inertly, with his life gushing out in a bright red stream over his shirt front. And Darrel FitzLee fell back over his chair and crashed to the floor, also, the sneering arrogance, the mad rage wiped abruptly from his face by the dark little hole that Steve O'Day had bored above the bridge of the clean-cut, aristocratic FitzLee nose.

Johnny O'Day was at the Crescent Bar as Steve, his brother, died smiling, on his feet in the saloon down the street. Johnny O'Day wasn't paying a great deal of attention to where Steve was that evening. Johnny, standing with his elbows on the damp mahogany, dreamily making wet circles with the bottom of his beer glass, was thinking about Mollie FitzLee, while a cowpuncher pounded out "My Wild Irish Rose" on the warped and battered piano.

The other two O'Days, Cass and Steve, never had that dreamy look. "That boy's different," Ma O'Day had often said when the three boys were younger. "Johnny'll never be like Cass and Steve. Catch them settin' around, dreamin' . . . the young hellions."

But Johnny didn't care, and he cared least of all now, for there, dancing in his mind, was the beauty and charm and grace of Molly FitzLee— remembering each gesture of her, the unconsciously imperious toss of her head, the easy way of her in the saddle, her smile as she turned to him, and the laughter in her brown eyes when they were riding that morning across the bottom pasture of the Double Loop, the range of the proud FitzLee men and their prouder women. Johnny O'Day was at peace, there in the Crescent Bar, and so he did not hear the roaring shots, smell the powder smoke that drifted over the big round table where cards and chips lay in passive mockery of the destruction they had brought about.

Dave Cole blew in the end of the belt gun, held it for a moment as he looked challengingly around at the witnesses. "Anybody got anything to say about it?" he demanded harshly. "All you men seen O'Day grab for his gun. He was honing for trouble."

The Double Loop men were already gathering around the spot, each one armed, each one plainly showing he was ready for trouble. It had happened so fast that many of the witnesses were not sure who had gone for his gun first. If there were any others who thought differently, they had nothing to say in the face of that show of FitzLee power.

A moment later all eyes were on old Major Jefferson FitzLee. He came slowly from the end of the bar, a tall, erect man in a black coat and polished boots, with his black hat tilted a trifle on his white hair and his carefully tended white mustache giving dignity and force to the thin arrogance of his face. His title of major won legitimately during the Civil War, his age and his prestige as head of the FitzLee clan, all helped to clear a silent, respectful way before him.

Silently the major stopped by the overturned chair, looked down at the body sprawled motion-lessly on the sawdust with the revolver still clutched in its hand. Silently he regarded his first-born, the pride and joy of his declining years.

His voice was stilted, strained, unlike the voice with which he usually spoke. He turned his head, looking at the silent men gathered about. "He's dead," he said slowly. His eyes grew bright with unspoken grief; his voice became shaky and high. "My Darrel . . . the finest boy who ever lived . . . killed by an O'Day! Their worthless father ran cows for the Double Loop when I first started the spread."

Major Jefferson FitzLee removed his hat, stood by his son's body. The light from the big oil lanterns overhead gleamed on the silvery whiteness of his head. His face worked for a moment. Not a sound was uttered in the big room as he lifted his head and spoke in a voice abruptly strong and terrible.

"Until the last male O'Day is dead," said Major Jefferson FitzLee in that terrible voice, "I will not stop striking them. They will all die for this thing they have brought upon me, and only then will I be ready to go, also." It was a prayer, a promise, an oath to the son who lay at his feet, a warning to all who heard, and an order to those who drew the FitzLee bounty.

The major clapped his hat back on his head, stooped, took the gun from the limp fingers of Darrel FitzLee. To Dave Cole he said tonelessly: "I think there are other O'Days in town this evening."

Turning on his heel, Major Jefferson FitzLee walked out of the place with his blue-veined hand gripping his dead son's revolver.

Dave Cole drew his lips back over his teeth as he looked around at his men. "He means it," he said. "Come on, boys."

They trooped after Dave Cole, hitching at their

gun belts, and, if there was law in the little cow town of Uvale that night, it was only the law the FitzLees were administering.

Cass O'Day was the eldest, the biggest, the strongest and the wildest. Built like a mountain oak, he towered a head above his other brothers and most of the men with whom he came in contact. He was always laughing, always gay, always reckless and daring.

That was Cass O'Day, the wild man like his father before him, a lovable man like that father, too, who bore no man enmity for long and who lived as the days came, laughing, fighting, playing, singing, and working with the fierce energy of two men on the Crazy Horse holdings of the O'Days.

You liked Cass O'Day or you hated him, and, when he was drinking heavily as he was tonight, you found it hard not to like him. Cass O'Day outdid himself at such times. His laughter was the loudest, his mood the most jovial, his songs the merriest of the merry company Cass O'Day gathered about him. And he had gathered many cowboys about him this evening in perambulations from bar to bar, with the Double Strike saloon housing them at the moment.

They were banked two deep at the bar about him, Anglo and Mexican, for Cass O'Day drew no line at friendship. Men from Uvale were there and men in from outlying ranches. When Major Jefferson FitzLee walked in the front door, Cass O'Day was just shouting jovially to the bartender for another round for the house.

Glancing over the heads of his companions, Cass O'Day spied the major just inside the door. "Major FitzLee!" he called. "What'll you have?"

The major did not reply. His face was set, stony. Under the white mustache his mouth was a hard, bitter line and the revolver was in his hand as he walked toward Cass O'Day.

Several men on the fringes of the group looked at the major's face and stepped quietly aside. It was the face of a dead man who walked with death.

Through the front door behind the major, Dave Cole walked in. His right hand was hooked carelessly in his cartridge belt near the handle of his gun. His bright black eyes swept the room watchfully. The men who followed him spread out warily. The FitzLee riders were all gunmen, all more or less touched by a degree of the FitzLee arrogance. A man couldn't be around the Double Loop long without soaking it up.

Cass O'Day saw none of that, or, if he did, it meant nothing to him. The world was a merry place and all men were friends of Cass O'Day this evening. With a sweep of his big arm he cleared a place around him.

"Let the major in here, boys!" he called. "Like

to have my neighbor at my elbow. Major, what'll it be?"

The major stopped two paces away. The way was clear between him and Cass O'Day. He was tall and straight, but now Major Jefferson FitzLee had to look up to Cass O'Day. Major FitzLee's voice had the toneless edge of a keen knife slicing down through newly butchered meat.

"Draw your gun, Cass O'Day," the major said.

Cass blinked at him. His smile grew broader. "Don't want to draw my gun." He laughed. "Good enough where it is. Cork's all we're drawing this evening."

The deep peal of his laughter rolled through the room.

The major said: "Draw your gun, Cass O'Day. I've come here to kill you!"

And no man who heard that voice, who saw the face that uttered it, doubted the truth of the words. Cass O'Day was suddenly standing alone at the bar with the major in front of him. And still he did not see what those about him saw.

Cass O'Day laughed. "Don't think I want to die tonight, Major," he said. "I'm buying this time."

For the third time the Major said: "Draw your gun, Cass O'Day."

Still smiling, Cass O'Day said: "Sure, if it'll make you feel any better, Major." He drew his gun, and, when it was out and lifted, Major Jefferson FitzLee emptied the remaining shots in

Darrel FitzLee's revolver into Cass O'Day's body.

The smile was still on Cass O'Day's face as he started to fall; the bewilderment that took its place as he went down hardly mattered. Cass O'Day was dead by then.

Dave Cole's wire-like voice cut through the dinning reverberations of the shots. "If there's any friends here that'd like to take up the argument, we'll be glad to accommodate them."

Friends were there—and so were Dave Cole's men, watchful, waiting. No man broke the stricken silence.

Major Jefferson FitzLee looked down at Cass O'Day's body. His hand was steady as he twisted the end of his white mustache, his voice almost absent as he turned away.

"There should be another one of them around town tonight," the major said. "The youngest. Cole, load this gun for me and we'll see."

II

Johnny O'Day finished his beer and drew a deep breath. The tinny piano with its haunting notes had taken him far away from the noisy clamor of the Crescent Bar.

The Double Loop headquarters of the FitzLees was a good two hours' ride away. Perhaps Mollie FitzLee was there, perhaps not. He hadn't seen her in town this Saturday afternoon or evening. She had said, laughing, that she would be at church in the morning, and that a bit of religion might be good for Johnny O'Day himself.

Mollie FitzLee had known he would come. Mollie FitzLee knew a lot of things about Johnny O'Day. It was plain in her look, her smile, her manner on those chance meetings down along Wild Turkey Creek that formed the boundary line between the Double Loop and the Crazy Horse for several miles.

For some reason or other they both had found it necessary to ride along Wild Turkey Creek a great deal lately. Johnny's mind was on Wild Turkey Creek when Steptoe Grafton came through the back room of the Crescent, saw Johnny at the bar, and limped hurriedly to him.

A bullet through Steptoe's right knee, in the dead of winter, had killed the horse under him and left him in two feet of snow, helpless, while the rustler who had fired it had ridden on to safety. Steptoe had been close to death under the bright still stars that bitterly cold evening when Johnny O'Day had found him, carried him to a Crazy Horse line cabin, and brought him through. But the leg had been stiff ever since.

Steptoe Grafton was breathing heavily; he had run from the Double Strike. His square face was pale and his eyes had a feverish look as he caught Johnny's arm.

"The FitzLees are lookin' for you!" Steptoe panted. "My God, Johnny, hell's to pay! Darrel an' Dave Cole shot up your brother Steve, an', before he died, Steve killed Darrel. The old major's gone crazy an' swore to wipe out all the O'Day men. He just walked into the Double Strike an' killed Cass, an' now he's lookin' for you with Dave Cole an' his men behind him. Get outta town if you value your skin!"

Thus tragedy and reality came to Johnny O'Day and wiped away the dream. They came so suddenly that he was stupid for a moment before the smashing shock of it.

"Steve dead . . . Cass dead?" Johnny said huskily, dully.

"Yeah."

Steptoe Grafton was almost sobbing as he told of Cass O'Day's killing. He shook Johnny's arm, as if to break the spell. "I'll never see a face in

190

hell like the major's! He thought a heap of Darrel. He's only thinkin' about killin' O'Days now. Fer God's sake, get goin', Johnny. Don't stand there lookin' like that!"

Johnny's face had gone hard, bleak. Lines sank in at the corners of his mouth and along his jaw. His gray eyes, which had been more used to dreaming than to stark, hard facts, lost their luster and became like two chips of stone in a face that seemed to have aged years in as many seconds.

"Steve and Cass . . . gone," Johnny whispered. "Killed by the FitzLees?"

So a bitter, grim maturity came to Johnny, the last of the O'Day men, at twenty-two. And as it came, Major Jefferson FitzLee walked in the front door of the Crescent Bar with Darrel FitzLee's revolver in his right hand.

Steptoe Grafton never saw the movement of Johnny O'Day's hand to his holster, but it moved; the gun was there in Johnny's hand, and Johnny was stepping out in the middle of the floor to meet the tall, aristocratic figure, stalking like the personification of doom toward him.

And if Johnny noted Dave Cole and the FitzLee men who came trooping in behind the major, no sign of hesitation appeared on the hard, bitter mask of his youthful face. Johnny's voice reached into every corner of the room as he stepped out.

"I'll kill the first man who reaches for a gun! Stop there!"

191

Neither Dave Cole nor his men had entered with their guns out. The order caught them unprepared. Dave Cole, at their head, took one look down the length of the room at the slightly crouching figure with the big Colt held on the door—and on Dave Cole—and Cole stopped short.

The legend of the O'Days' prowess with their weapons, if given a fair chance, bore fruit in that moment. Johnny O'Day was supposed to be the best shot of them all.

Major Jefferson FitzLee stopped, also. Johnny took a step toward him, sliding in the wary crouch that had taken him away from the bar. His thumb had hooked back the hammer of the single action Colt, his finger was tense on the trigger.

"I'll give you one step more, one move of that gun," said Johnny to the major, "and then I'll drop you! Understand me?"

Steptoe Grafton had slid behind the end of the bar. The other men in the room had scattered back against the walls, several even diving over the bar. Big Tim Doheney, tending bar, had ducked out of sight and come up with a sawed-off shotgun in his hands.

Major FitzLee spoke coldly: "I understand you, O'Day. I've come here to kill you."

Johnny grinned. His glance went past the major to the doorway where Dave Cole stood out in front, a perfect target.

Dave Cole saw the grin. No man knew that Dave Cole shivered in his inner self, but all men there saw him edge back a step against the men who crowded behind him. Johnny O'Day's grin was a death mask, bright with a sheer, cold threat that could not be doubted.

"Kill me?" said Johnny O'Day. "It'll take a better man than you and that gang of hired cutthroats behind you to kill me, old man. I've trapped an' knocked in the head better skunks than you'll ever be, or ever were. I hear that drunken pup of yours and that hired gun-toter, Dave Cole, killed my brother Steve tonight before he drilled Darrel. And so you hunted up Cass an' killed him to make it even, an' then came lookin' for me."

"I'm going to kill you," Major Jefferson FitzLee stated evenly.

Johnny gave him a bleak, cheerless grin. "Only a FitzLee would tote a conceit like that. Three for one . . . an' any of the three of us a better man than your pup would have grown into. You and your tribe have carried a high hand an' no one's cared enough about it to call you before. I'm callin' you now. Here's one O'Day you won't kill, an' won't run out of the country. I ain't killin' you because I'm not a butcher and I've got the drop on you. But from now on it's an eye for an eye. Now turn around an' walk out of here before I forget an' throw lead in you."

From behind the bar Big Tim Doheney spoke harshly: "I've got a thing or two to say about who gets shot up in here! The first man who starts trouble gets one barrel an' the second man gets the other barrel of this sawed-off. Johnny O'Day was a peaceable customer an' I'll help him stay that way, and be damned to all the FitzLee gunnies that can crowd in the door! Hear that, you hell-raisin' rannies? I'm throwin' in with Johnny O'Day on this!"

Those in the doorway moved uneasily. "Thanks, Tim," Johnny said without moving his eyes. "But stay out of this. It's my quarrel and I'll handle it."

Major Jefferson FitzLee did not even turn his head or give sign he knew Tim Doheney was there behind the bar.

"I'll die satisfied when I kill you, O'Day," he said with a deep breath.

"You'll die," said Johnny, "because I'll have to kill you. And they'll tell . . ."

Johnny never finished it aloud. But inside he went cold, empty, frightened. From the moment Steptoe Grafton had told him of Cass and Steve there had been no time to think. Johnny was thinking now—of Mollie FitzLee, with her wind-blown hair and her smile like no other smile that had ever been given Johnny O'Day. What would Mollie FitzLee think of the man who killed her father, no matter what the provocation? What would she think of any O'Day now?

"Get out of here, damn you," Johnny begged thickly. "I don't want to kill you."

And then Major Jefferson FitzLee lifted the gun in his hand.

A man had little time to think in such moments; life hinged on a fleeting second—and with Johnny O'Day it was not only life and death but the look in Mollie FitzLee's eyes which had to be acknowledged and reckoned with.

Major FitzLee was going to kill Johnny if possible, but if the major died first and Johnny lived, there would be nothing much to live for. You feel that way at twenty-two when you have dreams about a girl like Mollie FitzLee.

Johnny shot first. He had to. All the years of practice with that big belt gun were in the aim he took. The two guns spoke with one ear-splitting crash of sound. But Johnny's bullet struck first, as he knew it would.

Darrel FitzLee's revolver spun from the major's grip, firing wild. The major's hand was suddenly useless and bloody. He stood unarmed and defenseless in the middle of the floor.

Johnny shot out one light overhead in the same breath. The thunderous bellow of Tim Doheney's shotgun blotted out the other light as the big barkeep acted instantly. Tim Doheney would do a thing like that for a friend.

The sudden blackness hid all movement. It hid Johnny as he ducked over to the bar and ran for the door in the back of the room. It was the only way he could avoid killing Mollie FitzLee's father. Behind Johnny in the center of the floor the major made an effective barrier against any shots that Dave Cole or his men might have sent raking through the dark toward the rear door. And Dave Cole knew it.

Johnny heard him shout: "Get around to the back an' head him off! He won't have a horse out there!"

Johnny stumbled his way in the blackness to the back door, jerked it open, and lunged out into the cool night air.

Dave Cole was right. Johnny's horse was at the hitch rack in front. He had gotten it from the livery stable an hour or so before, meaning to ride after the supply wagon in which Geiger, one of the Crazy Horse wranglers, had started back to the ranch before dark. It would be suicide to go out in front, nor would it be much better to go wandering around town afoot. Dave Cole and his men would scatter and look for him.

Johnny ran to the right, where for one hundred yards there was no direct way to the street other than through the buildings. Cass's big bay horse should be out in front of the Double Strike. The bay had more speed and endurance than any other animal in the O'Day remuda. With a few minutes' start, the bay could stay ahead of any FitzLee man.

The most direct way to the street was through the Double Strike. Johnny opened the door, stepped into the back room, and stopped short.

They had carried Cass into the back room. He lay on the floor with a strip of canvas over him, boots and one hand visible. Cass, who would never laugh, never sing, never ride again.

Johnny said—"Cass!"—from a throat that was suddenly tight and hurting. He stooped, touched the still hand, and went on into the bar, swallowing hard at the lump in his throat.

Only a barkeep and several drunks were in the big room. Everyone else had followed the FitzLee men into the street to see what would happen. The barkeep recognized Johnny.

"Hell," he said, "I was waitin' to hear that they'd got you, too."

"No," said Johnny, "they didn't get me."

"I'm sorry, Johnny. It was murder. No other word for it."

Johnny nodded as he went to the front door. "This isn't the last of it," he said.

Few men were out in front. The center of attraction was farther along the street toward the Crescent Bar. But, as the search spread out, the crowd was spreading, too, filling the street as it drifted back toward the Double Strike. No one nearby at the moment looked like a FitzLee man.

The bay was there at the hitch rack, among a dozen or so other horses. Johnny walked out to it.

For a moment he wasn't recognized. Then, as he swung into the saddle, a man in front of the next building yelled: "There he is! Johnny O'Day! They ain't got him yet!"

The bay was out in the street when the first shot was fired and the first rallying yell raised for the FitzLee men. Johnny looked behind as he bent low and rode hard to the end of the street.

The crowd was rolling back. Men—FitzLee men, of course—were running toward the hitch racks, and a few scattered shots came after him.

His last sight, as the road curved through the one-story adobe Mexican houses on the fringe of town, was of horsemen gathering in the street.

III

Johnny slashed hard with the romel ends. The cool night wind sang in his ears; the legs pistoning beneath him drummed the road in unbroken rhythm. The bay was running like a race horse, and with the right handling he could keep it up for an incredible length of time. The FitzLees would have to kill their horses to get within shooting distance.

Two miles out, Johnny pulled into a walk, then to a stop. The silvery half disk of the moon hung high in the sky. Night insects droned and sang around him; the hard breathing of the bay pumped on the night. And that was all. Pursuit had vanished—or had not been there at all.

Puzzled, Johnny listened, watched. The minutes dragged. The bay breathed easier, and then began to move restlessly.

Dave Cole and his men should be in sight by now, if they were following. They had meant to follow. Considering all that had happened, there was nothing else for them to do, unless Major Jefferson FitzLee had restrained them.

The thought brought a cold smile to Johnny's lips. A bullet-shattered hand would not wipe out the hate, the inflexible purpose from the mind of that grim old man. He had set out to kill off the

O'Days. He would kill them off if possible. The fact that one of them had wounded him and gotten away would only make him more determined. The major's first order, Johnny knew, would be to follow, and keep following until the last of the O'Day boys had gone the way of Darrel FitzLee. And yet that order evidently hadn't been given.

Johnny rode on, more slowly, watching the road behind, stopping to listen now and then. He turned off the road onto a rough winding mesa track that cut back into the range country, spawning now and then a fainter track. One such track, miles farther on, ended at the little group of houses and corrals in the grassy draw among the foothills where the O'Day boys had lived and prospered.

Johnny's mother was there now, and Steve's wife and two kids, and the home riders for the Crazy Horse, who were to have gone in town the next Saturday night. It would be a sorrowful homecoming. Cass, Johnny thanked God devoutly, had never married. There would be no wife, no children to take the blow of his passing.

And, thinking that, he reined in Cass's big bay and listened. Far back the faint, distant roll of hoofs was vibrating on the night. Someone was riding hard after him.

Ahead one hundred yards a narrow wash cut through the low gravelly ridge on the left where only naked *cholla* cactus and a stunted juniper or so thrust up into the pale silver moonlight. But in the sandy side of the wash, silver-gray *chamiso* grew thick and high clear to the road.

Reining off into the wash, Johnny crowded the bay into the *chamiso*, so that they blended, rider and horse, into the harsh, dry growth. Only his head and shoulders were visible, and he could duck down out of sight if necessary. It would take keen eyes in the thin moonlight to see the tracks in the sandy bed of the wash and make anything of them, and keener eyes to pick out the motionless mass crowded into the *chamiso*.

Drawing his gun, Johnny tumbled in fresh shells and waited. The pounding hoofs were sweeping nearer every moment. Johnny frowned slightly. One rider only was coming there on the road— but, farther back, other riders were faintly audible now. The FitzLees must be coming, after all, riding so fast the slower horses could not keep up.

Johnny leaned forward tensely as the distant *crack* of a rifle drifted through the thin night air. An instant later the shrill, vicious keening of the bullet passed the head of the wash.

They were shooting at the first rider! He would be no FitzLee man, but it was a safe guess that those who followed him were. It became a running fight, for the rifle barked again and a second bullet *whined* across the mouth of the draw.

The lead rider shot back twice. He was very near now, galloping furiously. The rifle shots continued, closer each moment.

Johnny rode out into the open wash where the moonlight picked him out, stark and clear. The road was not twenty feet away. He was waiting there with his belt gun ready, and wishing he had a rifle, when the lone rider burst into view.

The rider was twisted in the saddle, firing back with a revolver. Two livid flashes burst from the muzzle of his gun as his horse plunged down the slight slope into the wash.

"Hi-yah!" Johnny yelled. And, for a moment, he thought the gun was going to be turned on him. The rider twisted sharply in the saddle, threw down on him, and the next moment reined savagely off the road in a shower of sand and plunged toward him.

Steptoe Grafton's voice came in a yell of hope: "Johnny?"

Steptoe's horse was dead-beat, lathered, heaving. Steptoe's voice was hoarse with urgency. And when Johnny answered the hail, Steptoe gasped out: "Three of the FitzLee men are comin' after me! Chased me outta town! I been ridin' like hell to catch you!" Steptoe dragged out his rifle. "I only got the shells that are in the magazine!" he panted. "I been savin' 'em in case I needed 'em durned bad!"

"Put it up," said Johnny. "This is my fight. Get back of me an' we'll see how three FitzLees act when a gun's thrown right in their teeth."

A touch of the reins as he spoke sent the bay

along the *chamiso* bank to the edge of the road. Not a moment too soon, either. The three riders were almost to the wash. They must have seen Steptoe turn into it, must have known he might possibly be waiting there for them. Superior numbers and the way Steptoe had fled ahead of them probably accounted for their recklessness.

They hit the wash riding hard after Steptoe and swung into it like a hunting pack hard on the heels of a fleeing animal.

"Put 'em up!" Johnny yelled.

He saw the first man, who carried a rifle, lurch around in the saddle and swing the long barrel at him. Johnny had the Colt on him as the gun started to swing. He squeezed the trigger; the gun leaped in his hand, and the rifle pitched down into the sand. The rider followed. The plunging horse bolted up the opposite bank of the wash.

The other two riders opened fire without stopping. Johnny felt the cold slap of a bullet across the upper muscles of his left shoulder. He heard Steptoe's gun bark beside him as he wheeled the bay out from the *chamiso*.

A second rider wobbled in the saddle, started to fall, dropped his rifle, and saved himself by grabbing the horse's neck as it galloped on up the wash. The third man followed, evidently unwilling to stand and trade shots with two men bold enough to spring this deadly ambush. Steptoe emptied his gun after him, swore disgustedly, and yanked his rifle out of the saddle boot.

"Let 'em go!" Johnny called to him. "No use killing when we don't have to. We're only trying to save our hides."

"I'd like to get all three of 'em!" Steptoe swore, dismounting awkwardly. Johnny was already down, leading his horse to the motionless figure sprawled in the loose dry sand. The man stirred slightly, groaned.

"Seems to have a little life in him," Johnny commented. He knelt—and the next moment grabbed quickly at the man's holster, wrenching the gun the FitzLee man had started to draw. Unbuckling the man's gun belt, Johnny tossed it over to one side.

"Just like a snake," he remarked disgustedly. "You've got to cut their heads off before they stop being dangerous. He's got a bullet in him an' he wouldn't have a chipmunk's chance if he shot me, with you standin' there to plug him. An' yet he makes a play for me."

"One hundred proof FitzLee cussedness," Steptoe grunted. "How bad's he hurt?"

"Stomach, I think," Johnny said, looking. "Mister, where'd it hit you?"

"Damn you!" the man gasped. "If I had a gun, you'd see!"

He was young, with a dark stubble on his thin cheeks and uncropped hair around his ears. A stranger. Men came and went on the FitzLee range, and most of them mixed little with the cowboys on the surrounding ranches.

Johnny said wryly: "You can't kill 'em and you can't cure 'em after they get a dose of the FitzLee high-and-mightiness. I reckon he'll last a while. Might as well bring him along to the ranch and do what we can for him."

"Leave him here," Steptoe said harshly. "You got other things to do besides fool with a rattler like that. Major FitzLee has sent his men to the Crazy Horse. He was out back of the building, holding his busted hand when he gave the orders to Dave Cole. 'Plug up a wolf's den,' he says, 'an' you'll keep him out in the open where he'll leave tracks.'"

"Damn his black heart!" Johnny said aloud. "He sent Dave Cole to my mother and to Steve's wife?"

"He's crazy tonight, Johnny. All he's thinkin' about is gettin' you. Dave Cole said somethin' about the women, an' the old major never turned a hair. 'They should 'a' spawned an' married better,' he says. 'It's their look-out. If you ain't man enough to do it, Cole, I'll get a foreman who is. Get there quick!'"

"Is that all he said?" Johnny asked.

Steptoe spat. "All I heard. I was standin' at the corner of the buildin' takin' it in. One of their men come runnin' an' bumped into me. I hit him in the head with my gun, dropped him, an' hightailed out front for my hoss. Some of the FitzLee men seen me comin' out. I guess they figgered I was goin' after you. I was just out of town when those three come after me. The rest have cut across country, I reckon, Johnny. It's rough ridin', but they'll make it before you do. An' they'll be waitin' for you. That's about what I was afraid of . . . you ridin' right into their guns. I did the best I could."

"I won't forget it," Johnny said gently.

He caught up the gun belt, picked up one of the rifles. Steptoe got the other out of the sand.

"You might as well take this fellow back to town," Johnny decided. "I'm going on to the ranch."

"I'm going with you."

"This isn't your quarrel. Somebody else is going to get killed before the night is over. It might be you. Go back to town and keep healthy. You've evened us up."

Steptoe Grafton's answer was gruff. "Who said anything about making us even? I'm goin' to tag along an' see the fun. Save your breath."

"You stubborn, pig-headed galoot," Johnny grunted. "I'm proud to know you. Help me get this *hombre* up over my saddle. I wouldn't leave any man here to die like that. Hold my horse."

Johnny heaved the wounded man up, mounted behind him, and with Steptoe riding at his side they took a more leisurely way along the narrow winding road.

"If Dave Cole and his men are at the ranch, they'll stick pretty close and wait for me to ride in to them," Johnny decided. "We'll turn off a couple of miles this side and circle around and drift in from the back. I want to get word to Mother and Steve's wife and get the hands together. It looks like this is going through to a showdown, unless Major FitzLee gets some sense."

"He won't," Steptoe said with conviction. "He's got it all figured out that Steve is to blame for Darrel's death, an' he figgers it'll take three O'Days to even it up. He'll keep on until he gets his three."

Johnny said heavily: "I wish I knew the truth about Steve. He wouldn't kill Darrel FitzLee or any other man without cause."

"He had the cause . . . there were five aces in that stud game. Darrel accused Steve of ringin' in the extra ace an' went for his gun. He had been drinkin' steady an' was ready to be ugly."

"Five aces? Hell! Steve never rung in an extra ace on any game!" Johnny snapped. "He gambled straight, always. And it wasn't Darrel FitzLee, either. He wasn't much good . . . but he had too much pride to cheat at cards. Give me the layout of that game as well as you know it."

"I was standin' behind the table," Steptoe said.

"Here's what happened." He described in detail all that he had seen.

"Who dealt?" Johnny questioned slowly.

"Dane Walker, the houseman. He had an ace showing, too, an' tossed it in the discard an' dropped outta the game."

"That," said Johnny, "sounds funny. I've seen Walker gamble. He can bluff as good as any man. If he had as much showing as Steve and Darrel, why didn't he stay in?"

"Well, he might 'a' knowed he didn't have a chance an' one of them did."

"Then, if he knew their cards, he was dealing a crooked game and knew there were five aces on the table. And if he knew that, he knew where they were."

"It don't make sense," Steptoe argued. "What'd Walker want to deal five aces for an' drop out? No percentage in that for him. He's cold-blooded. He wouldn't turn a hair to help his grandmother if there wasn't some cash in it for him."

"That's what I'm wondering," Johnny said. "What was in it for Dane Walker? What made it worthwhile for him to deal five aces just that way? He must have known it would end in trouble. Steve never bribed him, and Darrel FitzLee wouldn't. And if he did, he wouldn't go for his gun in the argument."

"I guess Dane Walker'll have to tell you that," Steptoe said.

And, grimly, Johnny said: "I think he will. Dane Walker dealt those cards to make trouble. If Darrel had been drinking and was ugly, Walker knew it. He knew there was apt to be shooting on the showdown. He must have dealt those cards to start the shooting. And he had a reason for doing it. I'll get it."

Steptoe said: "It'll take some persuadin' to make him talk."

"And that," said Johnny O'Day colorlessly, "he'll get. God help Dane Walker when I get my hands on him. He's cost me two brothers."

The wounded FitzLee man lay across the saddle like a sack of meal. Now and then he groaned weakly. But that was all. Johnny made him as easy as possible in the cramped position and paid no further attention to him.

Uphill and down they rode, at times pushing through thick piñon and pine where vision was limited to a few yards and dead branches cracked under the horses' hoofs.

Solitude hung about them like a thick cloak. Back in these isolated foothills, no men would be wandering at this time of night. A small army could not spread a line thick enough to intercept a casual rider who might be coming through at any point. The FitzLee men would be in close to the ranch buildings where that rider would have to come finally.

They gained the higher slopes and started to

angle down toward the little shallow valley that sheltered the Crazy Horse headquarters.

Steptoe Grafton stood up in the stirrups, looked ahead, exclaimed: "Do you see what I see, Johnny?"

The purple night sky over that crest was tinged with red. It deepened, brightened as they neared the top. Johnny, gripped by increasing forebodings, kept silent as he ducked branches and rode up the slope.

In the distance, in the home valley, flames were leaping to the sky over the home buildings, the corrals, and haystacks. Dwarfed by distance, the fire burned in soundless, awesome majesty against the background of the night.

The leaping flames were visible, the sparks spewing furiously up, the whole rising into a vast mushrooming column of smoke that towered high and drifted slowly off to the north on the night wind.

Johnny O'Day stared for a long moment. When he spoke, his voice was rough with a fury it had not expressed in all this night of tragedy and grief.

"Damn the black FitzLee heart! He's carried it to our homes an' our women! For this he'll go down on his knees and beg before I kill him . . . Mollie or no Mollie!"

"What's that?" Steptoe asked. "Mollie?"

"Nothing," said Johnny O'Day from a bleak

and hopeless face. "There's nothing, any more, Steptoe. All gone. I'm riding down to the houses. You'd better not come."

"I've got two rifles an' a handgun," said Steptoe Grafton. "A man who'd order that done, an' the men who'd do it, will get no more from me than they will from you. I'm ridin' down, too, Johnny. Let's go!"

IV

So they rode down together out of the higher foothills. The flames of Johnny O'Day's home, where he had dreamed away his boyhood days, lighted a path for them through the night. A blood-red path from which hope and dreams and laughter had been erased. There remained only violence, death, revenge.

Steptoe suggested without emotion: "Better chuck that skunk on the ground. He's only in the way now."

"No," Johnny refused. "He didn't help burn us out. He's a snake, but he's misguided. He came fighting an' he went down with a gun in his hand. I hate him, but he's not a FitzLee, and I won't leave him out here to die."

Steptoe said no more. He busied himself making sure there was no sand in the barrel of the rifle he had picked up. Johnny did the same as he pushed the bay faster and faster.

They came down out of the hills, two men riding against many. The first wild onslaught of the flames on haystacks and pitch-filled pine logs and lumber had slackened into the steady devouring destruction that would not stop until the rising sun glinted on the smoldering white wood ashes.

As they drew nearer, they could see mounted

men spaced at the edge of the red glare. The sullen *crackle* of flames gradually became audible, and grew louder as they topped the last wooded rise and looked across the gentle grassy slope to the burning buildings.

The haystacks were already dying down. The log buildings were sheathed in fire. The frame house—whose boards had been freighted forty odd miles by Johnny's father—was open to the night in spots, burning outside and in. The framework stood like a skeleton from which the board skin was peeling away, desolate, doomed, but stubborn with the lasting strength that Johnny's father had built into it in the high hope of his younger days.

The horsemen could be seen on the outskirts of the fire glare, dark and menacing as they moved restlessly about with rifles and handguns ready for trouble.

"Do you see any women?" Johnny asked. He didn't know that it came out a hoarse plea for comfort.

But Steptoe Grafton did. Steptoe's voice was heavy as he had to say: "No sign of 'em, Johnny."

Johnny dismounted, put the rifle on the ground, and dragged the limp form of the wounded man from the saddle to the ground, also. The man groaned as Johnny laid him out. He was still conscious.

"I've done all I can for you," Johnny said. "The

rest is up to the FitzLees. They'll find you here, for they'll be looking for their wounded when I'm through."

Johnny swung into the saddle again, lifted the rifle, sighted through the edge of the fire glare at the nearest rider, and squeezed the trigger.

Cass's big horse moved restlessly at the sharp *bark* of the shot, then stood still at the pressure of Johnny's knees.

Calmly, methodically Johnny sighted on another man. The second shot was low against the *crackle* of the flames before the first man leaned far out of his saddle, clutching vainly for support, and pitched down to the ground. The second man was reeling queerly when Steptoe Grafton opened fire with one of the two rifles he carried.

The watchful waiting of the FitzLee men became a sudden rout of confusion. Shouts of warning broke out. Horses reared, bolted as spurs were driven deeply. Other shots cut through the night from different points about the burning buildings. Another FitzLee man fell.

Johnny emptied the rifle, hurled it to the ground, drew a short gun from his hip. But for the moment, he had no use for it as he rode close to Steptoe.

"Hear those shots?" he called. "The FitzLee's aren't doing that! Some of our men must be around here!"

Steptoe snapped a shot at a vanishing target,

missed, lowered his rifle, and spat. "Good enough," he said. "We'll need 'em when Dave Cole gets his men together."

"We'd better move out of here," Johnny decided. "They're apt to close in on us. Most of the shots came from the other side of the corrals where that little rise of ground sticks out near the windmill."

He rode that way, keeping in the shelter of the trees. The firing stopped, and presently Johnny left the trees and rode through the open, past the windmill, toward the tree-covered tongue of higher ground.

"It's me . . . Johnny!" he shouted from cupped hands—and rode on for a moment not sure what would happen. Perhaps bullets would cut him down there in the open—as the FitzLee men had been dropped.

Then an answering shout—and a man showed himself at the edge of the trees with a rifle in his hand, and then another, and another. All afoot, waiting. As Johnny rode up, the rasping voice of Hank Stevens, top hand, greeted him.

"Glory be, you showed up, Johnny! We figgered it must be you an' the boys when the shootin' started an' we seen a couple of them dirty dogs get hit."

"Where's my mother an' Steve's wife and kids?" Johnny asked.

"On their way to that northwest line cabin,

Johnny. It's nearest. Geiger had just got back with the wagon when hell started poppin'. They came whoopin', yellin', an' shootin'. Stopped and fired the haystacks as they came. Your mother told Geiger to get the wagon over in the trees and told off a couple of boys to get Steve's kids outta the house. In half a minute they were on their way.

"Your mother knowed it was trouble, Johnny. She told us to get our rifles an' plenty of shells, but they cut us off from the bunkhouse. We got two rifles, three six-shooters, an' a few cartridges. That's, all. They run off the hosses an' our ridin' gear is burned. It's a hell of a mess. As soon as we saw the wagon on its way, I brought four of the boys back here to see what we could do. We was trying to figure out something when you started shooting."

Hank Stevens looked past Johnny and Steptoe. "Where's Cass and Steve? I figgered you'd be together."

Johnny dismounted. He looked at the four men who stood before him with the fire glare in their faces. Hank Stevens, tall, raw-boned, as honest and faithful as his angular, mustached face looked. A better man than most top hands would ever be. And Buck Sayles, chunky, cheerful, tireless in the saddle. Buck was not cheerful now. His round face was set, his eyes were squinting angrily.

The other two were Shorty and Slim Conners.

216

Two brothers. Shorty was the oldest, careful and methodical, in keeping with the gray that was beginning to fleck his black hair early in life. Slim, years younger, as gay and carefree as Cass had been.

All four of them were good hands, good friends. It was like that on the Crazy Horse. And now as they looked at Johnny's face, they fell silent. Johnny said tonelessly: "Cass and Steve are dead." And Johnny told them in his flat, colorless voice.

Slim Conners bunched a knobby fist. "I thought I made out Dave Cole in that bunch of riders, but I wasn't sure. Didn't seem like it could be. Johnny, we're with you."

Hank Stevens drew a deep breath. "There's only one way to deal with a locoed hoss," he said. "Kill it. I reckon we might as well get some ridin' gear together an' settle this quick. I've been here on the Crazy Horse eighteen years. I don't aim to be run off now. How about it, boys?"

"Hell, no!" they chorused.

None of the FitzLee men had appeared. The flames started to die down in solitude and quiet. "Funny," Johnny remarked presently. "Looks like they've run off."

Buck Sayles snorted. "They're three to one. Why should they?"

"They didn't know who we were," Johnny said. "I'll go see." He skirted the little valley in the

217

shelter of the trees that surrounded it. "They're gone," he said to his men when he returned. "Let's get over to the line cabin."

Johnny's mother was stooped with the years—hard years, many of them, but her eyes were dry, her voice steady as she faced them in the single, low-ceilinged room of the little cabin.

"My two boys are gone. Tears won't bring them back," she said, moving only the fingers of her work-worn hands. "I loved and raised them. I'm only an old woman now. This is a man's business. But Jeff FitzLee has a daughter and relatives left. I've only Johnny. Don't let them take him, too."

Hank Stevens spoke slowly: "They won't get Johnny, ma'am. I'll see to that."

Mrs. O'Day looked at the grizzled oldster. "I'll sleep better for that, Hank. You've never failed us yet. Now you men get out and let me put Steve's wife and kids to sleep. They . . . they need rest."

Outside, he directed the construction of a lean-to, a small fire to drive back the night chill. A huge pot of coffee helped. They talked long and earnestly before they turned in for a little sleep.

"The law won't help us," Johnny told them. "You all know the FitzLees had Douglas elected sheriff. He's their man. There'll be plenty to swear

Steve was in the wrong and that Cass drew his gun first. If we get tangled up with the law, we're licked. I'll be a dead man, our cattle will be run off, and the O'Days will be done for before anything can happen. That's all Major FitzLee wants."

Hank Stevens was troubled. "We ain't got enough men to whip the whole FitzLee tribe, Johnny. Maybe you'd better hide out for a while an' let the old man calm down."

"I'll settle with him in my own way," said Johnny. "Meanwhile, I've got other things to do. In the morning all of you take the women and kids over to the Bar Seven. It's twenty miles, but they'll be comfortable there."

Shorty Conners spat a thin brown stream of tobacco juice on a glowing ember. "What'll you be doing?" he questioned.

"I'm riding back to town, "Johnny said. "Steptoe Grafton's going, too . . . but not with me. I'm not healthy company right now."

Hank Stevens smoothed one end of his drooping brown mustache. "I'll just tag along an' watch how healthy it'll be . . . seeing as I made your mother a promise. Don't try to argufy me out of it, Johnny."

V

Sunlight lay bright on the dun-colored adobe walls of Uvale when Johnny O'Day and Hank Stevens rode into town. There was peace on the surface and brooding expectancy underneath. Uvale was holding its breath, waiting.

Their faces were impassive, but their eyes were watchful as they rode into the dusty main street. Johnny said quietly: "Lots of people in town this morning, Hank."

Hank spat to one side and brushed the backs of his hand across his mustache.

"Uhn-huh. Bunch of buzzards driftin' in. Some folks can smell trouble clean across a county."

Horses stood at the hitch racks; buggies, wagons had been driven into town. Men and women were in the open, and not all of them could have claimed to be coming to and from church. They waited, they talked in low tones, and, when Johnny and Hank rode calmly along the street, tension rolled up behind them like the sputtering advance of a burning trail of powder.

Voices stopped, heads turned. Those who would ordinarily have called a casual greeting held their tongues. There was something about the calm progress of the two riders that discouraged speech.

Hank Stevens said: "I wonder if some friend of the FitzLees'll take a shot at us?"

"Not in daylight, with everyone looking. See any of the FitzLee outfit?"

"Nope," said Hank, squinting around. "They're lyin' low or stayin' out of town. Looks kinda queer to me."

"I think," said Johnny, "that Major FitzLee will hold his hand until he's buried his son. They'll have Cass and Steve at Tucker Gantt's, I guess. I'll stop there first."

Tucker Gantt owned the livery stable, was the veterinarian, and at one side of the livery stable were the two adobe rooms used by Tucker Gantt, undertaker. Steve and Cass were in there. The business did not take long.

"Caskets," said Johnny. "The best you've got. Bring them to the Bar Seven."

Tucker Gantt was fat and bald and mournful. He did not try to hide his surprise. "The Bar Seven, Johnny? I figgered you'd want 'em brought to your home."

"They have no home to come to," Johnny said woodenly. "Bring them to the Bar Seven."

Outside, Hank called: "Johnny!" There was an urgency about the call.

"I'll see you at the Bar Seven," Johnny said to Tucker Gantt, and stepped hurriedly outside where Hank Stevens waited in the saddle.

Hank had swung his horse around and was

facing half a dozen horsemen who had just ridden up. The rifle that had been held loosely in Hank's gnarled hands now lay across one elbow, carelessly, so that its muzzle covered the street.

Hank did not take his eyes off the riders.

The rifle that Johnny had carried into Tucker Gantt's shifted the merest bit, ready for action, as he looked up into Dave Cole's thin, sharp face. The other men were FitzLee men, too. They sat warily in their saddles, looking from Hank Stevens's rifle to Dave Cole. No man put a hand to his gun, and yet Johnny had the feeling that they were waiting for orders.

Dave Cole grinned slyly. If he felt any emotion beside careless swagger, he did not show it.

"Put up the gun," he said, settling himself comfortably in the saddle. "This is Sunday an' we're in town on peaceable business."

Hank Stevens spat, did not take his eyes off the FitzLee foreman.

"It better be peaceable right now," Hank said calmly. "You're the first jasper I'll get, Dave Cole, if one of them damn' gun-toters behind you so much as wiggles an ear."

Dave Cole grinned slyly again. "They won't," he said. "We rode in on business. You two are free to hole up at the Crazy Horse an' make medicine."

Dave Cole's smile widened as he wheeled his horse toward a buggy that just then drove up beside the FitzLee men. Johnny O'Day, looking into the buggy, felt his heart turn over and go weak.

Mollie FitzLee was in the dusty buggy, her pale face like an ivory cameo. The same little, proud, imperious tilt to her head was there as she got out. They met on the walk. Mollie stopped. Her head came just to Johnny's shoulder. Her eyes were blue, clear blue, scornful, antagonistic.

"It's Mister O'Day, isn't it?" she said to him. "With a gun in his belt and a rifle ready to use."

"I'd probably be dead by now if I didn't have them," Johnny said bitterly.

She was no less bitter. "In here my brother is waiting to go home in a box. Killed by a card cheat. My only consolation is that Darrel killed him, too."

"Only a FitzLee would find an excuse for murder," Johnny said coldly, furiously. "Steve never cheated at cards in his life. And only a FitzLee would send gunmen to burn out women and children."

"What do you mean?" Mollie FitzLee demanded.

Dave Cole spoke from his horse. "You'd better go in, ma'am, an' let us handle this."

She silenced him with a gesture of her hand. Johnny was already speaking. "Last night we were burned out, houses, haystacks, everything. My mother and Steve's wife and kids are at the Bar Seven. They haven't any home."

Mollie FitzLee turned to Dave Cole.

"Do you hear what he is saying?"

"Yes, ma'am. Fancy tale, ain't it?"

"Did . . . did our men do anything like that?"

Dave Cole looked surprised, injured.

"Why, no, ma'am. Ask any of the boys here. We were chasing O'Day there, after he shot up your father. If there was any fire out to their place last night, most likely it was an accident."

Hank Stevens uttered a furious sound in his throat. "Durn your mangy hide!" he choked. "I got a mind to put a bullet in you for that!"

Dave Cole shrugged slightly as he looked down at Mollie FitzLee. "You see," he said. "They think gun talk covers everything. I'll have to warn him, ma'am, that, if he starts anything, we'll have to protect ourselves. Maybe you better go on inside."

"Watch it, Hank," Johnny warned. And he said to Mollie FitzLee: "There'll be no shooting here unless your men start it. Count noses when you get back an' see who's killed and who's wounded. No Double Loop man was wounded here in town, but several were at the ranch. They were taken away before this morning."

"I have seen no wounded men at the ranch, except my father."

"Somebody must have performed a miracle then," Johnny said with cold politeness. "Tell your father he'll hear from me."

None of the FitzLee men moved as Johnny

224

swung into the saddle. Mollie FitzLee was standing there quite still and white before Tucker Gantt's place as they rode off.

Hank Stevens spoke first. "She didn't seem to know we'd been burned out, Johnny."

"She wouldn't have cared if she had," Johnny said in the flat, dead voice. "They're all alike. All FitzLees."

"Kind of sweet on her, wasn't you, Johnny?"

"Once," said Johnny. "That was before I knew what they were like."

"Mmmmm," said Hank. "She talked a mite blood-thirsty, but I'll bet she wouldn't hurt a kitten. She's been upset . . . bad, since you last seen her. An' she don't know the whole story. Hell, Johnny, we don't know it ourselves. That's what we got to do here in town this morning."

"Are you taking up for her?"

"Nope," Hank denied. "I think she's a downright selfish, no-account chip off a proud, worthless block. She'd probably put a bullet in your back quicker'n Dave Cole. She looks to me like . . ."

"Shut up!" Johnny exploded. "I don't want to talk about her!"

"Don't blame you a mite," Hank agreed meekly. A faint smile touched his angular face.

Saddle gear *creaked* softly as they walked the horses down the street. Not so many people were visible now.

Hank chuckled softly. "They're huntin' cover.

Ain't just sure when the lead'll start flyin'." He cleared his throat. "Notice Dave Cole denied burnin' us out? Seemed mighty sure his men'd back him up, too."

"I was thinking about that," Johnny muttered.

Hank mused: "Funny she didn't hear it from her old man."

"You can't figure what a skunk'll do. I wonder where Steptoe Grafton is?"

"Ought to be around some'eres," Hank said. "He had a two-hour start. I guess he's took to cover to see what he can pick up about Dane Walker. That fish-eyed card shark ought to be out of bed by now, even if he does work half the night. Let's see if he's in Jack Diamond's. I need a drink, anyway."

They left their horses at the end of the long hitch rack, walked into the long cool interior. A hum of conversation died away, then started again, haltingly, as they walked to the bar.

Johnny said—"Howdy, Dan. Hello, Johnson."— nodding sober greetings to several he knew as he breasted the bar beside Hank.

They leaned their rifles against the bar front. In the mirror, Johnny could see the card tables. Dark stains on the floor marked the one where Steve had sat. Johnny sipped his beer slowly, knowing that men along the bar were watching his face in the mirror.

No games were running today. Dane Walker was

not in the place. Jack Diamond, the owner, was not there, either. But when the glasses were almost empty, Diamond walked in.

He was a pudgy man, not tall. Sloping fat shoulders supported a thick, powerful neck that seemed to rise straight up into the back of his head. Today his usual garb of shirt sleeves was replaced by a black Sunday suit, a lavender shirt, and a bright red tie.

Jack Diamond saw them, came to them, solemn, sympathetic. "Mighty sorry there was trouble in here last night, Johnny. I sure hated it. Have one on the house with me?"

Hank's surly refusal was growling in his throat when Johnny spoke calmly. "We'll have two beers . . . over at one of the tables."

"Two beers and a whiskey," Jack Diamond told his barkeep, and led the way over to a table.

As they sat down, he eyed the rifles. "You two look primed for trouble."

"We're not hunting trouble," Johnny said calmly.

The barkeep set the drinks down. Diamond tossed his whiskey off, ignored the chaser. His eyes were slightly squinting under heavily ridged brows. His nose, Johnny noticed, was thick at the base; his lips were extra thick, too. Usually they were smiling at customers. Now, sober, they were gross and hard.

Diamond tapped softly on the table with thick,

stubby fingers. "I'd have made a bet you were looking for trouble," he said.

"Nobody's asking you to bet," Hank grunted over his beer. "Why do you think we're on the wolf?"

Diamond shrugged, turned to Johnny. "Seeing what happened. You got a raw deal, Johnny. Your two brothers . . . your place burned out . . . if that don't call for a fight, I dunno. Maybe not."

"Who said our place was burned out?" Johnny asked calmly.

"Hell, it was, wasn't it? I've heard talk out on the street this morning."

"You're liable to hear anything," Johnny said. "By the way, where's Dane Walker? I want to ask him some questions about Steve."

Diamond shrugged again. "Hard to tell where Walker is. His time's his own, off work. He got drunk last night. I guess he's sleeping it off in his room over at Missus Green's boarding house."

As they left after a few moments, Hank snorted: "What'd you want t' drink with him for? He just wanted to find out what we was up to."

"Sometimes, Hank, it pays to give a man something to turn over in his mind. Did you notice he was all for egging us on into more trouble?"

"Uhn-huh."

"And I'm wondering how he knew our place was burned out. The ranch is too far from town for the fire to be seen. It's back where nobody'd

228

be riding by. Dave Cole and his men evidently just came to town . . . and they don't seem to be talking about it."

Mrs. Green's boarding house was a big, two-story frame building a block off the main street. Rooms and meals made it more or less a hotel. The fat, hospitable Mrs. Green was an institution who knew everybody and most things that happened in a fifty-mile radius.

She bulked in the doorway, radiating sympathy and helpfulness from her broad, kindly face. "I wisht I could tell you where Dane Walker was, but I can't," she told Johnny. "He didn't come in last night . . . his bed wasn't slept in."

"And you haven't heard where he went?"

"Not a word," Mrs. Green declared emphatically. "Mister Grafton was here about an hour ago, looking for him. I've asked several parties. Mister Walker usually takes Sunday dinner, and I wanted to know whether to set a place for him. Was there anything you wanted him told if he comes in?"

"Nothing," said Johnny. "We may be back later. If he comes in, don't tell him we were here."

On their horses once more, Johnny looked at Hank and Hank looked at him. "There's one for you to puzzle out," Johnny said. "What happened to Walker?"

Hank settled himself in the saddle and spat. "We can guess all day an' not get anywhere. I wonder where Steptoe went? He's been nosing around after Walker. Hell, ain't that him ahead there?"

Hank put two fingers in his mouth and emitted a piercing whistle. A horseman riding on the main street heard it, looked in their direction, and reined around toward them.

It was Steptoe Grafton, and he started talking as soon as he reached them. "I was lookin' for you two. The FitzLees are in town!"

"We seen 'em," Hank said. "They ain't on the prod just now. Find any trace of Dane Walker?"

Steptoe grinned. "I think so. Thought I was going to get a bullet in me when I got near him. It's funny, too. I can't figger it out. After tryin' at Jack Diamond's an' Missus Green's, a Mexican I know let on he might remember something if he had a drink to give him strength.

"I bought him a drink," said Steptoe, "an' he remembered then as how he was down with a load of red-eye behind Jack Diamond's place last night when Dane Walker was helped out the back door by Pablo Ruiz, the Mex roustabout. Walker was kickin' up a fuss, sayin' he wanted to go to sleep. Ruiz was tellin' him he was headed straight for bed, an' all the sleep he wanted. They headed off back of Jack Diamond's place toward Pablo Ruiz's house. That's why I figgered it was funny. How come Ruiz got so kindly he took Walker to his home instead of dumpin' him at Missus Green's, when it'd been easier and quicker to deliver him there? Ruiz ain't workin' today, either, so I rode over to Ruiz's house to pay a little call."

Steptoe sighed. "That scar-faced Mex met me at the door an' was about as friendly as a desert sidewinder. He didn't want no visits today. I made out as like I was a mite drunk an' insisted on comin' in. He shoved me out, an' cussed me out in Mex, an' drawed a gun, an' said he'd ventilate me for six generations back if I stepped in his door again. In fact," added Steptoe, "he just about let on he didn't want company today. So I gave him *buenos días, adiós, vaya con Dios*, an' clumb on my hoss an' went lookin' for you two."

Johnny said thoughtfully: "Ruiz is Diamond's man. He wouldn't make a move like that without Jack Diamond knowing it. Diamond told us he didn't savvy anything about Walker. He was lying. Hank, we'll ride over and see why Ruiz don't want any visitors today. Steptoe, you keep on around the block and make out you don't know us. Can't tell what's ahead. The less folks know about your helping us, the more you can do if we need you."

Following Steptoe's directions, they located the house without any trouble, a small, unplastered, single-story adobe set down in the Mexican quarter. The front door was closed. Johnny dismounted, knocked, and a moment later the door was opened part way and a voice snapped: "W'at you want?"

VI

Ruiz was a big man for a Mexican, heavily built, and there was more muscle than fat about him. His dark, flat face bore a purple scar across the left cheek. He was scowling.

"I want to talk to you," Johnny said. "Open the door."

"I don't want to talk to you!" Ruiz retorted. He started to close the door.

Johnny blocked it with his foot. "Don't try that," Johnny said. "You heard me say I wanted to talk to you."

Ruiz kicked at the foot. Johnny lunged against the door. It flew in, knocking Ruiz back.

"*¡Madre de Dios*!" the Mexican howled. "Get out before I keel you!" He lurched back toward the door, dragging at a gun that hung at his hip.

Johnny hit him on the jaw. Ruiz fell heavily on his back, but managed to get the gun out of the holster. Johnny kicked the weapon from Ruiz's hand.

Ruiz sat up, holding his sprained wrist. Glaring at the gun in Johnny's hand, he got to his feet, muttering. "W'at you want?" he demanded. "I don' ask for company. I don' want to talk. Me, I am home here resting an' you break in the door an' take over my house. For this I go to the sheriff."

"You can go to the devil, if it'll make you feel any better," Johnny said calmly. "No, keep your eyes off that gun on the floor. Where's Dane Walker?"

"I don' know. W'y you come here for Dane Walker? Thees my house. He don' live here."

"Who said he did? Open that door there an' let's see what's on the other side. Jump!"

Pablo Ruiz took one look at Johnny O'Day's face; the new face he had never seen before. Unwillingly, but hastily, he turned to the door and opened it.

Looking past him, Johnny said: "I thought so. Get in there!"

He prodded Ruiz into the next room with the gun barrel, prodded him over to the sagging wooden bed across the dim room, where Dane Walker lay on his back in the clothes he had worn the night before.

At first sight Walker seemed asleep. His hard face was relaxed. His breathing was regular. Johnny shoved Ruiz aside and shook the gambler. Walker stirred slightly, groaned faint protest, and slept on. Johnny slapped Walker's face, shook him roughly. It did no good.

"Hell!" said Hank disgustedly. "No man's got a right to sleep like that."

"Liquor never made him like this," Johnny stated. He swung on Ruiz. "He's drugged, isn't he?"

Ruiz shrugged sullenly. "I don' know. He come here to sleep."

"He isn't sleeping, he's unconscious," Johnny said. "Who told you to bring him here?"

"No one," Ruiz muttered.

Johnny stepped close, shoving his gun into the Mexican's middle. Ruiz backed off, his mouth opening silently.

"I've got a cure for a bad memory," Johnny said. "Talk fast, Ruiz, or the *señoritas* won't know that face when I get through with it."

"Before God, *señor*!" Ruiz wailed. "Of thees I don' know moch! *Señor* Diamond tell me to bring Walker here, an', eef he wakes up, to geev him drink from that whiskey bottle there. For that I get feety dollar, an' eef I let anyone es-see Walker, I get a bullet. *Dios*, w'at I do? *Señor* Diamond ees boss. Me, I am poor man."

Hank took a pint flask from a battered table by the bed, sniffed the red-eye in it.

"Let Ruiz take a couple of long drinks out of it," Johnny said grimly.

"I don' want to drink!" Ruiz protested.

"Guzzle it down," Johnny ordered unfeelingly. "If he won't take it peaceable, Hank, pour it down his throat."

Ruiz took the bottle with a shaking hand, tilted it, gulped three times before Johnny allowed him to stop. Choking, Ruiz pushed the bottle back at Hank.

"I'll go to the livery stable an' get a buggy," Hank said. "We'll ride Walker out on the mesa an' work on him. Hell . . . who's that?"

Hank swung to the wall where he had leaned his rifle. Horses had galloped up to the front of the house; men were dismounting quickly.

Johnny ran into the next room. His rifle was there inside the door. Just as he caught it up, the door burst in. Dave Cole entered, a gun in his hand, calling: "Ruiz!"

The Double Loop foreman saw Johnny in the same instant and whirled to face him, lips drawing back in a snarling grin. On his thin face murder was plain.

Three steps separated them. No time for the gun on Johnny's hip. He hurled the rifle straight out with both hands. It struck Cole's gun arm as Cole fired. The shot missed, and Johnny was on him, grabbing the gun, pushing it aside, wrestling Cole back against the wall beside the door-way.

A second shot blasted beside them. Hank Stevens bawled: "Stay out, all of you!"

That was all Johnny heard. He was trying to get the gun away from Cole. The Double Loop foreman was battling furiously to knock him back, to swing the gun muzzle in close. Johnny had both hands on it. Cole beat at his face.

Johnny stamped hard on the man's instep. Cole howled with the pain, went weak for an instant.

Johnny tripped him, twisted the gun arm hard as Cole went down.

The big Colt blasted again. The flash singed Johnny's sleeve, hot gasses drove through his skin, but the gun came away in his hands as Cole's arm was twisted almost to the breaking point.

Hank slammed the door shut. "I'll hold his dirty gun-toters outside!" he yelled.

Johnny hurled the revolver across the room, grabbed Dave Cole by the shoulder, and yanked him to his feet. And Cole, disarmed, robbed of the killing he had been so confident of, staggered back against the wall, suddenly pale.

Johnny moved toward him, breathing heavily. "So you're in on this with Ruiz and Jack Diamond?" he said.

Dave Cole licked his lips. "On what? I . . . I came here to see Ruiz. I thought you were out to shoot me."

"Shoot you?" said Johnny thinly. "That'd be too easy. I'm going to kill you with my bare hands. Lift your fists, Cole."

"It's two against one. I ain't got a chance."

"You've got more chance than our women had when you burned out the Crazy Horse last night," Johnny said, and he smashed Cole in the face.

Cole fought like a rat in a corner, viciously, savagely, with the knowledge that nothing else would do. He was strong, quick, and he had lied when he said he couldn't fight.

His fist whipped to Johnny's cheek, snapping Johnny's head back. Ducking in close, Cole struck him in the middle.

Johnny took it, and stood toe to toe and slugged with cold, savage blows that never stopped, no matter where Cole hit him. He began to grin—that bleak, death's head grin that had been on his face in the Crescent Bar the night before.

Before that grin Dave Cole gave back across the room, gasping for breath as he tried to protect himself. His cheek was cut; blood began to trickle from his nose; one eye started to close. Johnny walked into him, smashing, slugging until Cole stumbled, went down to a knee.

Johnny jerked him up, knocked him down again. He barely heard a loud pounding on the door as he hauled Dave Cole up a second time and swung hard with all his weight behind it to Cole's blood-smeared face.

The shock of the impact traveled clear to Johnny's shoulder. Dave Cole went down before it, and lay twisted on the floor without moving.

Dimly, as from a distance, Johnny heard a voice outside calling: "Open up or you'll get shot out!"

Hank Stevens turned a worried face. "It's the sheriff, Johnny," he said.

"Sheriff?" Johnny panted.

"Yep. Douglas. He come up while you was workin' on Cole. He wants to come in."

"He's been damned careful to keep out of all this so far. All right, let him in."

Hank raised his voice. "I'm goin' to open the door, Douglas. Come in without any of those FitzLee killers at your heels. We've took all we aim to off them."

Hank opened the door. He and Johnny stood watchfully with their six-guns ready while the sheriff stepped inside with his hands empty. Hank slammed the door again.

The sheriff was a commanding figure, towering over both of them. Someone had said he looked like a cannon and worked like a popgun. Despite the man's size his jaw was weak, his eyes were a watery blue, and he had been born to take orders. He had found the man to give orders in Major Jefferson FitzLee. Like most men who were weak in that particular way, Douglas had a certain measure of courage, and was stubborn.

Scowling, he said: "What's going on here? What happened to Dave Cole?"

Hank chuckled. "He got hit by a tornado."

Douglas took off his big tan sombrero. His nose was slightly crooked; his ears stood out from the side of his big head. "You two do that to Cole?" he asked heavily.

"I did," Johnny said.

"Where's Ruiz?"

"He's probably gone out a window," said Hank. "We ain't had time to keep track of him.

He was in the other room last I seen of him."

The sheriff stepped into the next room. He swore in amazement. "Ruiz is asleep in here on the bed with Dane Walker!"

"Asleep?" Hank marveled. "That stuff is horned lightin'. I guess he just can't stay awake on Sundays, Sheriff."

Johnny had followed the sheriff into the room. Pablo Ruiz was stretched full length beside Dane Walker, sleeping inertly. The sheriff tried to wake them both up without success. He sniffed the whiskey-tainted air.

"Drunk," he decided. "They can sleep it off here." He scowled at Johnny. "I came here for you, O'Day. I'm going to have to lock you up."

"Lock me up? What for?"

Douglas looked slightly uncomfortable. His watery eyes shifted away from Johnny's hard look.

"Lot of trouble last night," he said. "You shot Major FitzLee in the hand," Douglas added as an afterthought. "An' here just now you've gone an' beat up his foreman. I'm going to have to lock you up while I look into things."

From his post in the doorway, where he was watching the front door, Hank snorted: "You couldn't lock a jaybird on a piñon limb."

"Shut up, Hank." Johnny spoke curtly to the sheriff: "Kind of late looking up things, aren't you? How'd you know I was here?"

Douglas looked more uncomfortable. "I heard you was in town an' I been huntin' for you. Someone said they seen you ride this way. I'm straightenin' all this out as fast as I can. Meanwhile, I'm gonna have to lock you up for a little. Better come along peaceable because I got half a dozen deputies out there, an' Dave Cole has got three or four men that are armed. You can't get away."

Conscious that Hank was watching him, Johnny looked at the bed for a moment, and then nodded. "I'll go," he agreed. "I guess even you won't let anything happen to a prisoner in your jail. Hank, you can look after things." Johnny glanced at the bed again.

"*Mmmmm*," said Hank. "Sure. An' here's a bottle that might come in handy. Sheriff, you don't mind if Johnny has a little comfort in jail, do you?"

Hank held out the bottle from which Ruiz had drunk. Relieved that there was no trouble, the sheriff nodded as Johnny took the bottle and slipped it in a pocket.

"I guess it's all right," Douglas assented. "Gimme your gun, O'Day."

"Hank can take it, an' my rifle," Johnny said coolly. "Let's go."

And as Johnny walked to the door, he heard Hank warn the sheriff. "If anything happens to him, Sheriff, I'll settle with you myself. Don't forget."

"He'll be safe," Douglas promised. He was, it was clear, doing a thing that even he did not relish.

The sheriff stepped outside first, said: "All right, boys, there's no trouble."

They watched quietly while Johnny and Hank mounted, and then the men who the sheriff had deputized rode after them to the little red brick jail with its barred windows.

Hank saw Johnny into the jail, and then rode off. The sheriff locked Johnny in a cell, saying— "If there's anything you want, I'll get it."—and went out.

VII

Through the single barred window of the cell Johnny could see across several weed-grown lots a small section of the main street. People were gathering there, talking, looking toward the jail. But they were quiet; there was no sign of trouble.

Johnny rolled a cigarette and smoked thoughtfully. He was looking out the window when he saw the dusty buggy of Mollie FitzLee pass along the main street, headed out of town toward the FitzLees' ranch.

Behind her rode several armed men, but not as many as had come in with Dave Cole. Straining his eyes, Johnny was unable to see Dave Cole among them.

Through the rest of the day the jail was quiet. None of the other cells was occupied. Lon Marks, the regular deputy, brought a tray of food early in the afternoon. Marks was tall, gangly, loquacious. He lingered outside the cell while Johnny ate.

"How long do you aim to keep me in here?" Johnny asked.

"Derned if I know," Marks confessed, rubbing his chin. He lowered his voice. "Major FitzLee sent word to hold you. Douglas don't like it much, but he ain't gonna cross the old man. Don't let on I told you."

Johnny grinned thinly. "No danger. I figured that out already. I came along just to see what they were up to. I guess I'm safer in here than out dodging FitzLee guns."

"I reckon so," Marks agreed. "Douglas ain't skunk enough to let 'em come in here after you. He's keepin' everyone out."

The sun set; darkness fell, black, moonless. Marks and some cronies were playing poker in the jail hall. Johnny could hear them laughing, talking. He frowned, paced the cell. He hadn't counted on that poker game. He wondered if he had done the right thing by allowing himself to be locked up.

A gunfight at Ruiz's with the sheriff and the FitzLee men might have ended fatally for himself and Hank. Time had been needed to get at this mystery surrounding Dane Walker. By going to jail he had disarmed the FitzLees; they wouldn't be looking for trouble.

Hank's cautious voice under the window brought Johnny to the bars. "I got your hoss an' guns hid out near here. They took Dane Walker to the FitzLee ranch. Dave Cole drove him out in a wagon. Steptoe trailed it, seen it turn into the ranch road. I tried to get in to see you a couple hours ago, but Marks wouldn't hear of it. There's five of 'em playin' poker in there."

Hank's voice sounded worried.

"I never figgered on that poker game," he said.

"They're all armed an' keepin' the front door locked. I can't get in to 'em. Where's that bottle?"

"Here," said Johnny. "I've been saving it until you showed up. Sit down on the ground an' make yourself comfortable. I want my supper."

Banging on the cell door brought Lon Marks, and fifteen minutes later the food Johnny demanded.

"I'll get you a couple of blankets before I turn in tonight," Marks promised.

Johnny grinned at him. "Thanks, Lon. I sure appreciate all this. Here's something you can pass around the table out there. I won't be drinking tonight."

Lon Marks took the bottle with gratitude. "Mighty nice of you, Johnny." He grinned. "I guess five of us won't feel it much."

"You never can tell," Johnny said.

When Marks went back to the game with the bottle, Johnny calmly set about eating his supper.

"Nice food," he said through the window to Hank.

Hank's voice floated in mournfully: "Some jaspers has all the luck. I'm starvin' out here. Do you figger that stuff'll work?"

Johnny cocked his ear. "Not yet," he said. "Give it time. If I know those rannies, they killed the bottle soon as they got it."

Johnny finished the food, was halfway through a cigarette before the conversation about the poker table died away. The jail fell silent, still.

Hank had already slipped around to the front. A moment later glass *crashed*. Hank hurried into the cell passage with the jail keys, tried several, and finally unlocked the door.

"Good thing the front door wasn't barred," he said. "I'd have had to have got an axe. They had the keys inside the lock. I busted the window and reached into it. That bottle laid 'em low. We better hurry. The busted glass sounded loud."

Lon Marks and one of his cronies had leaned forward on the table and gone peacefully to sleep; another had slipped from his chair to the floor; the other two had gotten up, moved to different parts of the room before collapsing.

Hank and Johnny hurried outside and almost bumped into a man who was standing on the walk staring at the broken glass. Johnny drew his gun.

"Come here!" he said.

The man turned and ran instead.

"Might have known he'd do that." Johnny sighed. "Where's the hosses? The town'll be buzzing quick now."

Hank led the way across lots, behind some houses, and the horses were tied there in the darkness. They mounted, skirted the edge of town, and were soon riding through open country.

"I sent Steptoe back to the Bar Seven to tell our boys to meet us at Arroyo Vaco," Hank said.

"*Bueno*," Johnny said absently. "Hank, I've been wondering why Dane Walker was carried to the FitzLee place. Didn't it strike you funny that, if he stacked cards on Darrel FitzLee, he doesn't have any business around the Double Loop?"

"Hell . . . I never thought of that."

"Mollie FitzLee didn't savvy any wounded men around the place," Johnny mused. "They had all been taken away before we rode by our place this morning. They weren't brought to town or Steptoe'd've heard about 'em."

"Major FitzLee'd have 'em brought to the Double Loop," Hank said flatly. "His cussed, ornery pride wouldn't let him do anything but take care of 'em."

"I'm trying to think," Johnny said, "where Dane Walker could be on the Double Loop. Not in the bunkhouse, not around the main house. They wouldn't cart him out to any of the FitzLee kin."

"If Dave Cole took the Double Loop road, he pretty near headed into the home place," Hank said.

"Seems so," Johnny agreed. "Wait . . . I've got an idea. Back up the draw north of the Double Loop bunkhouse there's a couple of old log cabins that were used by married hands. My father an' mother lived in one the year before they quit the Double Loop an' took up land. Those cabins haven't been occupied for years, except when there's too much company around the ranch. Maybe . . ."

"I think you got an idea there, Johnny."

It took an hour and a half to reach Arroyo Vaco. By then the thin moon washed faint silver over the countryside. A cautious hail issued from a clump of piñons to the left of the road.

"Hank . . . Johnny!"

"All right, boys," Johnny answered. Seven riders came forth—Slim and Shorty Conners, Buck Sayles, Geiger, Steptoe Grafton, and two men from the Bar 7. The Bar 7 had mounted them all well; every man had a rifle and six-gun.

Buck Sayles said: "We got going soon as Grafton brought word. Tom Winston on the Bar Seven wanted to bring all his outfit. After talkin' with your mother, he was for joinin' in to clean out the FitzLees. But she wouldn't let him until you sent word. They're ready to ride if you want 'em."

"Not tonight," Johnny said. "We've got too many now for what we've got to do. We aren't cleaning out the FitzLees. It's more like robbing a hen roost. But you boys all know that, if shooting starts, it'll be for blood. Don't take any chances. I'll ride ahead. I know the Double Loop. We'll keep off the road. Most likely they've got guards out. I would, if I had as much oneriness on my conscience as old man FitzLee has. Let's go."

They rode for another hour after that, nine men, drifting through the faint moonlight almost silently. The Double Loop stretched far and wide, and night and distance gave all the cover needed.

247

Johnny circled wide, coming in from the north. They were fully two miles from the Double Loop home buildings when they saw the twinkle of lighted windows. Johnny let his men gather around him there and said: "We'll cross an arroyo about a mile ahead. Hank an' Buck an' I'll go on alone from here. The rest of you drift slowly after us. If you hear any shots, ride in fast."

The arroyo was shortly behind them. Johnny led his two companions on, watching landmarks carefully. He halted presently on the crest of a little ridge and pointed down through scattered piñons.

"The cabins are down there along the edge of the draw," he said under his breath. "I'll ride down alone. Don't come unless you hear my whistle."

Hank protested dubiously. "I don't like it, Johnny. Your hair ain't worth a shed rattler's skin if you get caught out here alone."

"If the major keeps his word, it isn't anyway," Johnny said. "They think I'm in jail. I'll be all right."

And he rode on alone, down through piñons into the grassy draw where two low, log cabins bulked darkly against the gentle slope on the left. Beyond the widening mouth of the draw the lights of the FitzLee home buildings could be seen plainly. The two log cabins were unlighted, silent. Unoccupied, Johnny guessed as he rode up to the nearest one.

"*Hi-yah!*" he called softly from the saddle—and the next moment he straightened as an answer came from the other cabin, fifty yards beyond.

"That you, Dave?"

"Uhn-huh," Johnny answered, riding toward him.

From the dark door of the second cabin a disgusted voice spoke as he rode up. "This guy Walker has got the shakes. He says he's got to have a drink. He wants to go back to Uvale. He's disturbing the wounded. Say, where'd you get that hoss? . . . you ain't Dave Cole!"

VIII

Johnny had swung to the ground, was almost to the dark doorway where the speaker was standing. The man leaped back inside, started to slam the door, and Johnny drove his shoulder against it and knocked it back.

The next moment a gun roared in the blackness inside; the bullet clipped his leg; he fired at the flash, and plunged inside. A second shot clipped the hat from his head. He fired again.

A gun *clattered* to the floor. The dull *thud* of a body followed, then a groan. "Walker!" Johnny called.

From his left a husky voice answered. "Here! Who is it?"

In the darkness Johnny heard dull stirrings, but no one else threatened. He struck a match, saw bunks against the walls in which badly wounded men were lying. Walker was sitting on the edge of one bunk, peering into the match light uncertainly. As the match went out, Johnny caught the gambler by the neck and hauled him to his feet.

"Here . . . what's the matter? Leggo me!" Walker protested.

He had come out of the stupor, was shaky, but

in full control of his senses. And fear was in his voice.

"D'you know me?" Johnny said, shaking him. "Johnny O'Day! Steve O'Day's brother! What about that fifth ace in the card game?"

"Don't savvy you," Walker gulped.

"Damn you!" said Johnny. "You ran in that ace. Jack Diamond's drugged you. Dave Cole brought you out here to the Double Loop. What's the answer? I'm ready to kill you quicker than Steve got his."

"Take that gun outta my belly," Walker gasped. "Is this the Double Loop? They wouldn't tell me. Said I'd been on a big drunk."

"You were drugged. Diamond did it. Ruiz had you in his house until Dave Cole brought you out here in a wagon."

Hoofs pounded up to the front of the cabin. Hank called: "Johnny!"

"All right, Hank! I've got Walker!" Johnny shoved the gambler toward the door with a gun in his back. "We'll take you out where you'll talk with a rope around your neck!"

In the doorway Walker looked at the two other men and wilted.

"I'll talk," he said thickly. "If they drugged me, they're stackin' the cards on me. I won't stand for that. Jack Diamond paid me a hundred dollars to work that fifth ace in the game. I don't know why he wanted it. I gamble for a living. If the boss

251

wants a crooked game, it's his business. I think Dave Cole knows something about it. He an' Jack Diamond have had their heads together a lot lately."

"I knowed it," Hank Stevens said with satisfaction. "What are we gonna do now, Johnny?"

From his horse Buck Sayles spoke sharply. "Men comin' hell-bent for leather from the ranch. Mighty near a dozen of them! They heard the shots!"

"Put a rifle bullet over their heads," Johnny ordered. "Walker, climb on your belly across my hoss an' hang on."

Buck Sayles's rifle spoke. A loud yell drifted from the mouth of the draw. As Johnny swung into the saddle behind Dane Walker, he saw a dark bunch of horsemen scatter at the mouth of the draw and race toward them. Little stabs of red dotted their progress, and the shrill *whine* of flying lead zipped viciously through the night.

"This way!" Johnny yelled. He spurred behind the cabin, galloped up the sloping side of the draw into the trees. Buck Sayles and Hank rode close, ducking, dodging the low branches.

"Buck!" Johnny yelled. "Ride on an' find the rest of the boys. Keep shootin' so you'll be followed. Take the rest of the fellows an' draw these FitzLee men over toward the Crazy Horse! Don't mix with 'em more'n you can help."

"OK!" Buck answered. He bent low and rode

hard as Johnny reined sharply off to the right, galloped to a thick clump of trees, and drew rein. And not a moment too soon. The rush of the FitzLees was drumming hard toward the spot.

They passed close, dim shapes in the moonlight riding hard after the fast-receding reports of Buck Sayles's revolver. When the last man was past, Johnny rode out of the cover and headed back toward the draw.

"Where you going?" Hank questioned.

"In to have a talk with Major FitzLee," Johnny said calmly.

Hank jerked around in the saddle. "Are you loco, Johnny?"

"Never have a better time than this, Hank. They branded Steve as crooked, an' I'll nail that lie in their teeth tonight. You'd better go after the rest of the boys."

"You're crazy an' I'm crazy for lettin' you," Hank declared. "We'll nail it together."

They rode down out of the trees at the mouth of the draw and headed for the bunkhouse and the big, sprawling adobe castle of the FitzLees on beyond. Built haphazardly through the years, the big house enclosed a huge open patio where flowers grew, water trickled into a rock-bottomed pool, and a tall cottonwood towered to the sky.

As they drew near the front of the building, a man stood forth in the moonlight, hailing them.

"Major FitzLee wants to know what happened?"

he called. "Where's Dave Cole?" He carried a rifle in his hands.

A slender figure stepped to the balcony railing overhead. Moonlight shone on a white Spanish shawl, and Johnny knew who it was before Mollie FitzLee's clear voice carried through the crisp, still air.

"Who are they, Barker? Isn't that a wounded man across the saddle?"

Johnny rode toward them without answering, wondering how many more armed men were there in the shadows.

And then the angry voice of Major FitzLee issued from a dark doorway at the back of the balcony.

"Tell those men to speak out or stop where they are!"

Hank husked from the corner of his mouth: "I can stop that rifle first shot."

"Wait," said Johnny. He raised his voice. "It's me . . . Johnny O'Day! I've come to see you, Major! Call off your gunmen, for I'm comin' in!"

Silence for an instant. Then Major FitzLee's voice, terrible, bitter. "Shoot that man down, Barker. Juan . . . Jennings . . . Morse . . . out in front with your guns!"

And Mollie FitzLee's cry: "Dad . . . you can't do that! It's murder!"

Johnny's belt gun was in his hand before Mollie FitzLee spoke. The rifle on the terrace had snapped up toward him. A door banged open at the back of the terrace in the same instant. And Hank's rifle spoke at Johnny's side as the FitzLee man shot.

Johnny felt the hammering smash of the bullet against his left side, knocking him awry in the saddle, driving breath from his lungs. He saw the FitzLee man stagger, drop his rifle, with it *clattering* on the terrace flagstones, heard Hank's exclamation of satisfaction, then alarm.

"Drilled his shoulder clean! What's the matter, Johnny? He get you?"

"No!" Johnny retorted as he spurred his horse to the terrace, up, *clacking* on the flagstones, riding down, putting to flight the wounded man.

Johnny breathed again. He threw the dizziness off with a terrific effort of willpower and came down out of the saddle with a rush, groaning with the wave of pain through his side as he landed hard on his feet. He plunged to the back of the terrace, yelling at Hank, who was out of the saddle then, too.

"Bring Walker in!"

Under the balcony the shadows were black. Fire laced from them as his weaving rush hurled him into the shadows.

Johnny shot as he came; his bullet went home somewhere behind the flash. He followed the stumbling retreat of the man through the unlighted front door. He was so close that he bumped into the other when the man collided with a third man in the darkness.

A startled oath burst from the third man as Johnny found a head with his left hand and clubbed it hard with the heavy revolver. He stepped aside quickly as the body went down, heard the third man, at arm's length away, cry: "Morse, are you plugged?"

Johnny reached the speaker in a step, jammed his six-gun savagely into the body. "Throw down your gun!" he ordered.

He had guessed about the gun—and he heard one strike the floor at his feet. He said: "Turn around! Lead me to Major FitzLee!"

No threats were needed. The gun muzzle was enough. Johnny caught an arm with his free hand, shifted the gun as the other turned quickly, and moved ahead of him to a door. And the door, opening, let light about them from the big, high-ceilinged living room.

Square-hewn beams crossed overhead. A balcony ran across one end. Deer heads, mountain lion, and bobcat skins were on the walls, and the massive furniture had been handmade by men on the FitzLee payroll.

A pock-faced Mexican with a gun in his hand had just reached the bottom of a straight flight of steps. Halfway down the steps, Major FitzLee was hastening, with his right hand swathed in bandages and a gun in his left. And behind him was Mollie FitzLee. Johnny called over the shoulder of his prisoner: "Hold that Mex before I kill him!"

Major FitzLee did not have to speak. The Mexican stopped, backed up a step, looking for cover or an avenue of escape. And Major FitzLee ignored the order and descended the stairs deliberately, tall, erect, proud, and without fear. He reached the bottom and said: "O'Day, you have broken into my house. I expected something like this. But now that you are here, I'm going to finish what I failed to do last night."

"Dad! Please!"

That was Mollie, pale, afraid. She caught her father's arm. He shook her hand off, and in that moment Hank Stevens spoke behind Johnny.

"Here's Walker, Johnny. And if that old coot gets reckless with his gun again, I'm goin' to kill him myself."

Mollie stepped in front of her father, her cheeks suddenly blazing. "Killing . . . shooting!" she cried passionately. "It's cost me my brother, brought unhappiness and sorrow! You men can't do any more of it! You can't!"

"Mollie, get out of the way," her father said calmly. "O'Day, what is that man Walker doing here?"

"I brought him," said Johnny. "Brought him from one of those log cabins beyond the bunkhouse where he was hid. He slipped the fifth ace into that game. I brought him here to tell you."

Major FitzLee stood very still. For the first time uncertainty showed about him. "Walker, what about it?"

Dane Walker was haggard, shaking. "I dealt it, all right, I guess," he muttered. "Jack Diamond told me to."

"Then," said Major Jefferson FitzLee in a voice suddenly hoarse, "Steve O'Day wasn't playing a crooked game?"

"No," said Walker.

Before Johnny's eyes Major Jefferson FitzLee seemed to wilt, to become less erect, to lose the pride that had cloaked him through life.

"Then Darrel and Steve O'Day . . . and Cass O'Day . . . ?" He broke off, swallowing.

"All of them," said Johnny bitterly. "Because the FitzLees were too damned proud to listen to reason. My two brothers gone, our place burned out, the women run off in the night."

"I had no houses burned, O'Day."

"Two days ago I wouldn't have given you the lie on that," said Johnny. "But you were heard ordering Dave Cole out to the Crazy Horse. And I found your men there watching the fire. I shot 'em up. The wounded are in the cabin where I found Walker."

"Dad, you told me it didn't happen!" Mollie's voice was abruptly bitter, too.

Before her father could answer, men ran into the hall. Johnny barely had time to step back as Dave Cole burst into the room with four men.

"We heard the shots!" Cole exclaimed. "It's all right now, Major. O'Day's men have been run off. Our men are following them."

"Where were you, Cole?"

Dave Cole looked startled at the cold question. "Over beyond the bunkhouse," he replied after a moment's hesitation. "At the cabins in the draw."

"Who have you got in those cabins?"

"Several boys who got shot up chasing O'Day last night," Cole said unwillingly. "I put 'em there. Didn't want to bother you while you were laid up with that hand."

"Cole," said Major FitzLee ominously, "why did you burn out the O'Day place?"

"I didn't," said Dave Cole suddenly. His glance went to Dane Walker. "This man has been drunk," he said. "He doesn't know what he's doing or saying."

"Let him be," Johnny snapped. "You wanted him out here bad enough to bring him in a wagon today after your boss had the sheriff lock me up."

"I had the sheriff lock no one up," Major FitzLee stated flatly.

"Then," said Johnny, "Cole used your name to get me out of the way while he got Walker out here. Walker was drugged after the card game last night. Jack Diamond and Cole here are working together."

"I see," said Major FitzLee. The muscles in his jaws were ridging. He was holding himself calm only with visible effort. "You . . . Jack Diamond," he said to Cole. "A crooked game is rigged between my son and Steve O'Day. I gave you orders to ride to the O'Day ranch and wait there for O'Day's arrival. You went . . . and burned them out, and kept it quiet. Today you gave false orders to the sheriff in my name, and bring this gambler out here and hide him on my place. Presumably so he won't talk. I'm not a fool, Cole, although I've been blind and hasty. What were you up to?"

Dave Cole grinned. "Nothing . . . now," he said. "I see you're going to fire me. I'll go laughing, Major. I never did like you, with your nose in the air all the time. Jack Diamond and I wanted the O'Day place. Never mind the swearing. I'll be laughing at you every time I hear a gun go off. You mighty near pulled our potatoes out of the fire. Think it over after I'm gone. I'm in the clear on all this." Then, turning to the Double Loop hands who had come in with him, he said: "Time to go, boys." And he turned to follow them out.

"Wait, Cole!" The command stopped the foreman's departure. "I've thought it over," Major FitzLee said forcefully. "You've cost me my son and driven me to kill an innocent man. You've stripped me of my pride and left me shamed and grieved. Stand still!"

"Don't do that!" Dave Cole shouted, stumbling back as he lifted his gun. Mollie FitzLee screamed as the two men fired together, almost into each other's chests. Johnny reached her as she fainted.

As he swung her up in his arms over the dead bodies of her father and Dave Cole, Hank Stevens's voice emerged from the reverberations of the shots. "Johnny, you was lucky the major didn't cut loose at you with his left hand. Too bad he ain't alive to see how clean he drilled Cole."

Johnny said as he turned toward the stairs: "Handle it, Hank, while I take care of Mollie. She's going to need us. You'd better send for my mother. She'll come."

And Johnny O'Day walked up the stairs with Mollie FitzLee in his arms, Mollie FitzLee, whose smile was like no other smile he had ever seen. Grief was still on his features as were the years that had come in a night, but his eyes were dreaming once more, seeing things beyond the present, and a new peace was smoothing out the hard bleak lines from his face.

Last Waltz on Wild Horse

It was perhaps his ambivalent relationship with Marguerite E. Harper, his agent from the beginning, that had somehow been a requisite for Ted Flynn to keep on writing as long as he did. Harper had persuaded him to concentrate on writing Western novels to be published as original paperbacks by Dell Books rather than for pulp magazines that were coming to an end. However, his sixth novel did not adhere closely enough to the Dell paradigm, and it went unsold. Ironically it was one of the best stories he had ever written. "I also have one unsold Western book, the last I ever wrote, which did not sell," Ted wrote Phyllis Hatch on May 6, 1974 from Castro Valley, seven years after she had inherited the Harper Agency from her sister. ". . . That ended my writing career, and good riddance, say I. Almost forty years of beating the tired brain is enough. And if you don't think so, you should have suffered through *all* those years, as did MH, who I am sure is probably keeping an eye on things, and would like to prod me sharply quite often. Sun is out, blossoms are out, the lemon tree will have lemons the year around again after the freeze-killed mess last year. Hummingbirds are humming, and the horses are running. What could be nicer?" That last novel titled *Night of the Comanche Moon* was first published in 1995 as a Five Star Western. Except for "So Wild, So Free", unpublished until its appearance in *The First Five Star Western Corral* (Five Star Westerns, 2000), "Last Waltz on Wild Horse" was T. T. Flynn's penultimate Western short story, and the last one to be published during his lifetime. It appeared in *Zane Grey's Western* (2/53), a digest-size pulp magazine published by Dell that would cease publication with the January, 1954 issue.

John Egan was not dancing tonight. His right leg, still bad from the gunfight in which the outlaw Teller brothers had escaped, kept him on a wall chair in the long, merriment-filled hall. His wife was dancing. His daughter was dancing, too often, with Dick Starr, his young and increasingly cocky deputy. Starr would have Egan's job, and daughter, too, after the election, Egan suspected. Six years ago he'd guessed settling in Elkton would end about like this.

Six years ago the Nuckols gang had killed the former sheriff, and urgent telegrams had reached Egan in Wyoming. Elkton needed an iron-willed peace officer. Elkton wanted John Egan of the legends, Egan of the wild boomtowns and roaring camps. And when Egan had come, and cleaned up the Nuckols bunch, Elkton had elected him the new sheriff.

His wife had wanted it, Egan recalled. Wanted relief from endless worry about Egan's safety. Wanted a peaceful home for young Ann, already leggy and fast maturing. He'd warned Ruth dryly the public never remembered long. Local men would soon eye the sheriff's job again. As they were now.

The real trouble was Sam Quinby, influential

rancher and horse trader, from whose mountain pastures last year Egan had culled eighteen stolen horses.

Quinby had produced bills-of-sale, and finally, furious and shaken, had grudgingly admitted to being tricked by slippery strangers. Now Quinby and friends would probably make Dick Starr the next sheriff. John Egan was half crippled, wasn't he? Not even a local man! Send him back to his stale boomtowns and fading camps. . . .

Six years made a difference, Egan thought ruefully now, watching the dancers. A man got older. Home took roots. This time he didn't want to move on. Egan looked up without expression as Sam Quinby finally stopped to greet him.

Quinby was elegant tonight in frock coat and polished boots. His sandy beard was trimmed and combed, his smile was broad, and his question genial. "Egan, how's the leg?"

"Still on," said Egan blandly. "How's horses and slippery strangers?"

"Business," said Quinby, "is slow." His eyes were cold.

Egan's eyes were colder as Quinby moved on, shaking hands. They understood each other. Quinby was a thief and knew Egan knew it. Dick Starr wouldn't have culled those eighteen horses, Egan thought restlessly. Dick was honest but friendly and lacking in suspicion.

Outside now it was blowing and raining, but no

one in the gaily-decorated hall cared. Egan sat with his thoughts, and he was probably the only one who sensed trouble arriving with Ira Burch.

A small man with thin, harried features, Burch owned a hard-scrabble homestead and large family back in the Clear Creek hills. He came in alone out of the wet night almost furtively, and sidled to Egan, pulling off a wet, yellow slicker.

Burch's question was hurried, secretive. "How much reward on the Teller brothers?"

Egan sat very still, lean and brown, tough and composed, his shock of black hair streaked with gray. A smolder kindled in his boring blue gaze. Losing the Teller gang, and getting crippled while doing it, was a rankling failure Sam Quinby and friends were exploiting.

"Sit down, Ira." And when Burch gingerly took the adjoining chair, Egan said: "Better'n three thousand on both the Tellers. Why?"

Burch's Adam's apple slid nervously in his leathery neck. "Even a small chunk of reward'd help, the way kids eat an' get sick. . . ." His voice trailed off dispiritedly.

Egan nodded. "Know where they are?"

"The Tellers an' two other men pushed forty, fifty horses into Big Blue Cañon at sundown. They never seen me back in the brush."

Egan said—"Horses?"—and glanced at the far end of the hall where Sam Quinby stood by the orchestra platform, elegant, impressive, respectable, and influential.

"Horses?" Egan murmured again, and remembered his bad leg and looked out on the dance floor.

Dick Starr and Ann were dancing this schottische, also. Young Starr was taller than Egan, hard-flanked and friendly-looking. Ann, like her mother, had a sweetness of brow and a gay sparkle. She was laughing up at Dick.

"Wait at my house," Egan said abruptly to Burch.

Then Egan sat quietly. Big Blue Cañon was not far from the high mountain meadows of Sam Quinby's horse ranch. Easy to guess where the Teller brothers were heading with rustled horses. If Dick Starr broke it up tonight, Sam Quinby might lose his enthusiasm for Dick as sheriff. Egan smiled faintly.

The schottische was ending. His wife came, flushed and smiling, to the chair Burch had vacated. Her escort was pudgy Len Hall, owner of the Emporium.

"I get older an' stiffer and Ruth gets younger," Len complained gallantly, blowing ruddy cheeks.

When Len walked away, Egan murmured: "Still the prettiest one." Ruth touched his hand. Her brown hair had more gray than Egan's black hair. Otherwise, Ruth hadn't changed much, Egan thought. He said casually: "Tell Dick I want him to help me home."

The old apprehension about Egan's safety darkened in Ruth's look. "I saw that man come in. Trouble?"

"Not for us. Sam Quinby, maybe." He watched Ruth go, wondering how her laughter and faith and pride had persisted through all the years he'd been a notorious peace officer, hired usually when other men refused the risks. These six years as Elkton sheriff had been by contrast quietly peaceful. And Ruth was grateful.

A gay varsoviana was beginning as Egan, cane in hand, limped awkwardly from his chair. He stopped several times for casual, low-voiced talk with different men, and finally reached young Dr. Marsden.

"Time for this leg to make a ride, isn't it?" Egan wheedled.

Marsden put on his sternest look. "You can't dance tonight, either, John." Then young Marsden's grin was encouraging. "Patience. You might wreck that knee for good if you force it. Do I have to ride herd on you?"

Egan chuckled ruefully. "You've herded me too much now." He saw Dick Starr coming and limped to meet him. They went out together into the blowing rain.

Dick's question was airy. "Something wrong?"

"Ira Burch saw the Teller gang pushing horses into Big Blue Cañon before dark."

Dick whistled softly. "Rustled horses?"

"They ever have any others? And it's not far from Big Blue Cañon to Sam Quinby's horse ranch."

Dick said with amusement: "You'll pin something on Sam Quinby yet, won't you?"

"Probably." Egan wondered if it mattered to Dick, who had never mentioned Sam Quinby's talking him up for sheriff. But Dick had been getting cockier lately. "We'll get the Tellers," Egan said tersely. "You'll have to do it. I'll drop you at the livery stable. Come to my house. Don't talk."

Pacing Egan's slow limp on the wet boardwalk, Dick protested: "Tonight?"

"When else?" Around the corner, Egan hauled himself into his buggy and backed the team out of the solid rank of wagons, buggies, and saddle horses. Dick Starr sat beside him silently. "When you sight 'em," Egan advised, "don't hold back."

Dick sounded absent, unenthusiastic. "Telling me to bring 'em in dead?"

"You know what I mean."

"You've said it enough." This was some of Dick's new cockiness. He was deputy, but not too seriously.

"It's kept me alive," Egan reminded brusquely. "I've tried to tell you. Never give a killer a chance. He'll kill you."

"Will he?" muttered Dick politely, and Egan held back a caustic retort. From the livery barn,

Egan drove to his small frame house. Ira Burch was waiting in the kitchen. Other men Egan had contacted at the dance rode into the backyard and stamped into the kitchen.

Fred Stovel was short, bandy-legged, and active. Carl Flegge was stolid, muscular, with red veins netting his face. Bob Joyner and Harley Cook arrived together, both big men. Then Dick Starr came in, shedding his slicker off broad shoulders and sizing up the gathering.

Ira Burch had put a pitch-pine stick into the range and heated the big coffee pot. They swigged black coffee while Egan talked from his chair beside the kitchen table.

"Only one good place to hold horses in Big Blue Cañon tonight. Wild Horse Flat. You can ride by Dry Bone Creek, over Baldy Knob, and take that old mustang trail down into the upper cañon, and come at 'em from above."

Dick protested across his coffee cup: "That mustang trail is dangerous on a night like this."

"It's the sure way to surprise 'em," Egan insisted. He watched Dick's jaw set silently.

Bob Joyner said bluntly: "We need more men."

"There's enough of you," said Egan flatly. "Last time, a bigger posse gave it away. Someone warned the Tellers. No one but us knows this now. Back out if you like."

"Guess not," Joyner decided.

Dick Starr eased the heavy shell-studded belt

on his hips. His quizzical grin ran over the five men. "Egan's calling this dance. We'll waltz the Tellers around Wild Horse Flat. Let's go."

Cocky, Egan thought uneasily. The iron, somehow, was missing. From the kitchen doorway, he watched their mounted, slicker-clad figures, hats pulled low, vanish in the blackness and pelting rain. He limped to the range for more coffee, and sat down, nursing the cup.

The house was quiet. The range fire popped softly. Rain tapped the windows, bringing memories of other bad men Egan had known, braggarts, blusterers, and quiet ones. And the worst of them had a common trait: they killed callously, efficiently. John Egan had been more efficient. He had lived.

Did Dick Starr really understand that, Egan wondered, and wished he knew what Dick was thinking. It was more than Dick, more than Egan and the job now. It was the way Ann looked at Dick, the gay, eager giveaway in Ann's smile.

Egan lifted his head as the front door opened. Ruth and Ann came into the kitchen. They were damp and deceptively cheerful.

Egan answered their unspoken question. "Dick's off on a little business."

Ann carried cups to the coffee pot. She looked flushed and tense. "Is it dangerous?"

"Never can tell." He was aware the legends of John Egan had never been a matter of pride for

272

Ann. Violence appalled her. Now Ann's low voice held a note of accusation.

"Isn't it more dangerous when wanted men think the law may kill them?"

Egan pushed his cup back. "Been talking that way to Dick?"

"Is it wrong?" Ann asked defiantly.

"No. But an outlaw who's killed other men is already dangerous. Let Dick do his own thinking. He's got plenty of it to do."

Ann said tightly: "You're jealous of Dick, aren't you?"

Her mother's hurried question headed off Egan's mild outrage.

"John, why should Sam Quinby send his foreman from the dance hall after you left with Dick? And when the man came back, why should Quinby leave quickly with him? I came home to tell you."

Egan said softly: "So Slippery Sam didn't miss a move. Means he knows the Tellers are due." Egan picked his cane off the floor and heaved to his feet. "Ruthie, get my work duds."

Worried, Ruth asked: "What is it?"

"The Tellers are in Big Blue Cañon with rustled horses. Dick's trying to trap them. Sam Quinby's evidently trying to stop it."

Ruth said apprehensively: "You can't try to ride there with that knee." Ann was biting her lip. Egan eyed her and caustically reminded: "The Tellers kill and argue later. Dick'll have to match them. If he doesn't, he's a boy on a man's job. Just the kind of sheriff Sam Quinby and the Tellers would like."

Ann looked confused and frightened. Ruth eyed her worriedly, and then silently left the kitchen to help Egan get ready.

A little later Egan rode into the night alone, another bowed figure in slicker and down-pulled hat. In the horse shed, Ruth and Ann had helped him saddle the sorrel by lantern light. Ann had said unsteadily under her breath: "Don't let them kill him."

" 'Course not, honey."

Ann had seemed comforted. John Egan had promised her. Egan of the legends and roaring towns. Ann was learning, Egan thought morosely, what her mother had lived with. Rain gusts whipped the slicker. Egan rode with a long right stirrup, putting little weight on the stiff knee. It was awkward, tiring. His thoughts settled professionally on the Teller brothers.

Luke and Joe Teller had known prisons. They'd killed. In their forties now, the Teller brothers were hardened and dangerous. The men with them would be as bad.

Around midnight, Egan forded Dry Bone Creek. The rushing, soupy current, swollen by the rain, made the horse stagger and lunge. The rain was slacking to fitful spits. Egan rode hunched and silent. Dick Starr would probably wait until daybreak. If the Tellers had been warned, Dick and his unsuspecting men would ride into waiting guns. Bob Joyner, Egan thought, had been right. Too few men in the posse.

Over Bald Knob the trail was muddy, slick. It climbed into the dense blackness of jack pine stands. The wind soughed overhead. The uneasy trees dripped. In daylight, this higher country gave glimpses of grandeur. Tonight Egan rode through chill, damp blackness to the timbered ridge that dropped in treacherous shale slopes to the great gash of Big Blue Cañon. Pain throbbed now in the bad knee as he dismounted clumsily and tightened saddle cinches and tried to remember details of the hair-raising descent.

Hauling into the saddle, Egan put the nervous, reluctant horse to the narrow downtrail and gave the beast its head. At his left, yawning black space whipped the imagination. Close to his right stirrup, the dripping cañon wall lifted sheer. Small stones, dislodged into space, fell far and long.

Strain sawed at Egan's forced calm. Not seeing it was worse than the hair-raising reality of daylight. This pinned a man against black space, at the mercy of imagination. When the horse suddenly slipped, Egan was already braced tautly.

The beast floundered. Shod hoofs struck red sparks from stone. Egan grabbed the saddle horn, expecting a frantic slide into space. Then, miraculously, the horse got certain footing, and braced, shivering.

Carefully Egan gathered the reins and spoke soothingly. He was sweating. He wondered how Dick's men had fared on this wet, treacherous descent into the upper cañon. Presently the horse moved hesitatingly and continued slowly down, and down. At long last it reached the bottom. Egan was weak.

Here in the deep cañon the rushing pour of Blue Creek growled through the darkness. The trail was not wide but it was safe. Egan breathed deeply, smiled wanly. It had been close up there. Close.

Sometime later, miles down the cañon, Egan's horse suddenly nickered.

Another horse nickered in the blackness ahead. Egan was already reining back hard, reaching inside the slicker. Should have had the gun ready in his hand, Egan knew disgustedly.

Must be the posse. . . . Then Egan heard the soft trample of many horses moving up the cañon toward him. A suspicious demand blurted from the dark at him.

"Who is it?"

Egan said: "Sam Quinby. Which one are you?"

"Make a guess, you lyin' . . ." A gout of orange flame blotted the rest of it.

Egan fired at the flash and battled an impulse

to duck. Reining the startled sorrel hard, he half emptied the gun in one tearing burst of sound— and saw no other muzzle flashes replying.

Through the slamming echoes, he heard the horse herd stampeding back down the cañon. Distant yells came from men who'd been pushing the herd. They couldn't have met the posse, so Dick Starr hadn't come this way.

A man on the ground ahead sighed gaspingly. Egan's gun covered the spot. "Where you hit?"

The reply was mumbled. "Belly. . . ."

"Which one are you?"

"Teller . . . Joe. . . ."

Egan said coldly—"So you were tipped off?"—and got no reply. "If it'll cheer you, I'm shot, too," Egan said. "Hang on if you can, and I'll hang you later."

Joe Teller's horse trampled uncertainly in the darkness as Egan rode past warily. He reloaded the half empty gun, his anger blazing. Dick Starr had let the job down like a man eying election. Like a man wanting Sam Quinby's approval. It came to Egan now how much he'd wanted Dick to handle this right. Wanted the best for Ann. Only the best would be a matter of pride to Egan and deserving of Ann.

The Tellers, Egan guessed, believed now the posse blocked the upper cañon. Overhead cloud scud above the high cañon rim was letting through the first faint dawn. Daylight soon. Egan reached under the slicker to a torn flesh wound in his left hip. Blood was oozing into the boot.

Bad knee, bad hip, he should turn back, Egan knew. An odd feeling of being completely alone now caught at him. He thought of Ruth at home, waiting out one more night, and felt less alone.

Cottony mist drifted along the cañon bottom where Egan cautiously rode. He shoved the handgun into the slicker pocket and pulled the carbine from its scabbard under his right leg and jacked in a shell.

The hip hurt. Pain needled the bad knee. Egan pulled his mind off that and watched the cañon ahead. An elbow-like bulge where the cañon bore off to the left held Wild Horse Flat, several acres of grass and scattered trees. Sluice miners, long gone, had left a rotting cabin.

Egan had it figured. If the Tellers were escaping, some of the abandoned, stampeding horses would stop at the flat and start grazing. Mist hugged the flat and wraith-like trees lifted out of it. The rush of the creek bore off to the left, against the towering rock of the cañon side. Horses were grazing on the flat in the mist, and Egan smiled thinly and rode toward them.

His only warning was a belated glimpse of one more horse off to the right by the fringing brush. A saddled horse, reins tying it to the ground.

Derision howled in Egan's mind at his carelessness. Joe Teller's saddled horse was far back up the cañon. No one else had been shot. This horse had an owner close. Then Egan sighted the man at the back corner of the old cabin, a vague, solitary figure in the drifting mist, leveling a rifle.

Egan ducked to the sorrel's neck, heeling the animal into a lunge that might put one of the grazing horses between them and the rifle. With sound legs, he would have rolled off Indian-like and fought with the sorrel for a shield.

The *snapping* rifle report drove a bullet soddenly into the running sorrel and Egan had to roll off helplessly anyway. The derision howled again. This shot had come from the brush near the saddled horse. Not from the man at the cabin.

He hit the wet earth, sprawling and tumbling. It beat him helpless with shock and hurt in the hip and knee. He stopped on his side, the slicker peeled up around his hips. Egan of the legends caught cold and helpless. And by the Tellers, a second time.

Yards away his horse was down, kicking. *Dropped the carbine, too* was Egan's groggy thought as he rolled over painfully and pushed up. He saw the indistinct figure running through the mist at him, rifle ready. This, Egan bleakly guessed, was the time he didn't ride home.

He sat up, bracing with a hand on the ground, watching the man half circle him, to keep Egan and the trail upcañon in sight. The Wanted dodgers, Egan thought, had been clear enough. Medium height—brown mustache on a wide, beefy, stubble-roughened face—ears larger than average, batting out a little.

"Luke Teller," Egan said, noting the man's grimy saddle jacket, collar turned up, heavy cartridge belt strapped outside.

The reply was rough and panting. "Where's Joe?"

Egan said succinctly: "Shot. You want to surrender?"

"You John Egan?"

"Yes."

Luke Teller got his breath back and gazed up the cañon. "Where's your posse?"

"Got it in my pocket," said Egan coldly. "You and the rest want to surrender?"

"Just me waited for Joe. So Joe's dead?"

"Wasn't when I left him. He'll probably hang if he lives."

Luke Teller looked up the cañon again. He was calm now. "One sure thing, Egan, you won't hang Joe. Or anyone."

Egan was trying not to watch the second figure off there in the mist, vague and crouching a little as it moved toward them. A Teller man wouldn't come like that. It looked like Dick Starr. Egan was afraid to believe it was Dick Starr coming from the cabin corner.

He thought Ruth would understand what he was going to say. They'd lived it together. Sitting awkwardly on the soggy earth, bracing with a hand, Egan spoke coldly.

"It's always the law hangs them. Which is why fools like you hide out and stay on the run. You shoot a few men, but you never kill the law. So someone like me gets you finally. Want to bet I won't hang you or shoot you?"

"Hell of a bet," Luke Teller said. He was peering through the mist, trying to see what was up the cañon. He looked at Egan and brought the rifle centering on Egan's chest. A vagrant thought moved his mouth corners in a grimly humorous smile. "How's this for a bet, Egan? I'll live longer than you will."

"Dead man's bet," Egan said. "You wouldn't collect." He could feel the harshness in his throat. This was more than talk; this was the barely delayed pressure of Luke Teller's finger on the hair trigger.

Teller's grin was jeering, and Egan looked at the face, not the rifle, and said coldly: "I'll bet a thousand you aren't fool enough to shoot. I'll write it an I.O.U. Sam Quinby can collect and pay you. If you win."

Luke Teller was amused. "How'll you collect, Egan, if you win? I'll be dead."

"I'll share in the rewards on you."

A vague puzzlement filled Luke Teller's stare.

Slowly Egan swallowed. Couldn't help it. He'd always known what to do. Now, suddenly, he was uncertain. Was this right? Was this the thing to do?

Like moves ahead in a desperate checker game, his thought flashed over it. If Dick Starr was slow or inclined to words—if Dick even hesitated—then Luke Teller was going to kill Dick.

Then the gun still in Egan's slicker pocket would be out, covering Luke Teller, who would die or hang later. But Dick would be dead, traded for Luke Teller.

Would Ann understand that the law sometimes had to work like this? That it wasn't a question of Egan's life, but whether Luke Teller got away to kill again?

Egan knew. All her life Ann would not understand. Each time she looked at Egan, Ann's mute accusation would not understand.

Puzzled, irritated, Luke Teller demanded: "What are you tryin', Egan?"

For hanging, Egan thought. Wanted for hanging! A man lived with his beliefs and held to them. Coldly, calmly Egan said: "Shoot me and your gun will be empty. Look behind you."

Coldly Egan studied the disbelief struggling on the wide flat face. Luke Teller moistened his lips. His side-step was sudden. His glance swiveled over a shoulder. Dick Starr was not far off in the mist now. In frantic haste Luke Teller swung his rifle.

Egan shouted—"Now, Dick!"—and clawed at the slicker pocket.

Dick's rifle snapped its sharp, clean report against the dawn. After a moment, Egan let his gun stay where it was.

Dick looked shaken as he ran up and kicked the rifle from Luke Teller's prone, groaning figure.

"First time I ever shot a man," said Dick thickly, stepping to help Egan lurch up. "And the last, I hope."

"It won't be," said Egan shortly. "Goes with the job. This kind would take over the law if not stopped. You won't last long as sheriff until you learn it."

Dick looked puzzled, then his shrug was careless, his slow grin amused and admiring. "That talk of Quinby's? Why, there's only one John Egan. I'll never be that good. Ann and I are planning to ranch. We were settling it at the dance tonight when you pulled me away."

"That so?" Egan muttered weakly. He was feeling light-headed anyway, from losing blood into his boot he guessed. He fought an urge to sit down again and said caustically: "That don't excuse you from taking the easy way here. If they hadn't run into me an' thought I was the posse, they'd have had you. Where's your men?"

Dick's jaw looked stubborn again. "That mustang trail was too dangerous at night. The men are holding prisoners. Three of the gang rode into us thinking the posse was up the cañon behind them. They were too surprised to fight. They said Luke Teller waited here at the flat. So I came after him."

Egan was feeling more light-headed, and a little proud, suddenly, of Dick. "Came after him alone? You a rancher!" Egan took a deep breath. "Well, you had one waltz with the bad ones to remember." He knew he was going to sit down and he reached for Dick's steadying hand.

"Go ranching," Egan said weakly, trying to sort out his thoughts. "You and Ann. You'll live longer. A man likes this work or he doesn't last."

Dick said—"Yes."—humoring him.

"Got the Tellers. Got you an' Ann settled," Egan muttered, trying to think. "Something else, though. . . ." He captured it with immense effort. "Among the men you caught . . . one of Sam Quinby's men?"

"His foreman," Dick said.

Egan nodded, satisfied now to be light-headed, with Dick handling the rest of this.

"Something for Sam, too," Egan murmured. "We called it for him, too . . . last waltz for Sam. Tell him so, Dick, an' lock him up."

Reflectively, contentedly Egan sat down on the wet ground again. Ruth, at least, he thought, would understand and be a little proud, even if Egan was packed home this time and tossed in bed.

Acknowledgments

"Showdown in Blood" first appeared as "Hot Gun Town" in *Dime Western* (5/48). Copyright © 1948 by Popular Publications, Inc. Copyright © renewed 1976 by Thomas Theodore Flynn, Jr. Copyright © 2008 by Thomas B. Flynn, M.D., for restored material.

"Spawn of the Gun Pack" first appeared in *Western Story* (4/19/41). Copyright © 1941 by Street & Smith Publications, Inc. Copyright © renewed 1969 by Thomas Theodore Flynn, Jr. Copyright © 2008 by Thomas B. Flynn, M.D., for restored material.

"Last of the Fighting O'Days" first appeared in *Dime Western* (10/1/34). Copyright © 1934 by Popular Publications, Inc. Copyright © renewed 1962 by Thomas Theodore Flynn, Jr. Copyright © 2008 by Thomas B. Flynn, M.D., for restored material.

"Last Waltz on Wild Horse" first appeared in *Zane Grey's Western* (2/53). Copyright © 1953 by The Hawley Publications, Inc. Copyright © renewed 1981 by the Estate of Thomas Theodore Flynn, Jr. Copyright © 2008 by Thomas B. Flynn, M.D., for restored material.

About the Author

T. T. Flynn was born Thomas Theodore Flynn, Jr., in Indianapolis, Indiana. He was the author of over 100 Western stories for such leading pulp magazines as Street & Smith's *Western Story Magazine*, Popular Publications' *Dime Western*, and Dell's *Zane Grey's Western Magazine*. He lived much of his life in New Mexico and spent much of his time on the road, exploring the vast terrain of the American West. His descriptions of the land are always detailed, but he used them not only for local color but also to reflect the heightening of emotional distress among the characters within a story. Following the Second World War, Flynn turned his attention to the book-length Western novel and in this form also produced work that has proven imperishable. Five of these novels first appeared as original paperbacks, most notably *The Man from Laramie* (1954) which was also featured as a serial in *The Saturday Evening Post* and subsequently made into a memorable motion picture directed by Anthony Mann and starring James Stewart, and *Two Faces West* (1954) which deals with the problems of identity and reality and served as the basis for a television series. He was highly innovative and inventive and in later novels, such as *Night of the Comanche Moon* (Five Star Westerns, 1995), concentrated on deeper psychological issues as the source for conflict, rather than more elemental motives like greed. Flynn is at his best in stories that combine mystery—not surprisingly, he also wrote detective fiction—with suspense and action in an artful balance. The psychological dimensions of Flynn's Western fiction came increasingly to encompass a confrontation with ethical principles about how one must live, the values that one must hold dear above all else, and his belief that there must be a balance in all things. The cosmic meaning of the mortality of all living creatures had become for him a unifying metaphor for the fragility and dignity of life itself.

Center Point Large Print
600 Brooks Road / PO Box 1
Thorndike, ME 04986-0001 USA

(207) 568-3717

US & Canada:
1 800 929-9108
www.centerpointlargeprint.com